HELL ON THE RHINE

Recent Titles by Duncan Harding from Severn House

Writing as Duncan Harding

Assault on St Nazaire
Attack New York!
The Finland Mission
The Normandie Mission
Operation Judgement
Sink the Ark Royal
Sink the Bismarck
Sink the Cossack
Sink the Graf Spee
Sink HMS Kelly
Sink the Hood
Sink the Prince of Wales
Sink the Scharnhorst
Sink the Tirpitz
Sink the Warspite
Slaughter in Singapore
The Tobruk Rescue

Writing as Leo Kessler

S.S.Wotan Series
Assault On Baghdad
Death's Eagles
The Great Escape
Kill Patton
Operation Glenn Miller
Patton's Wall
The Screaming Eagles
Sirens of Dunkirk
Wotan Missions

Battle for Hitler's Eagles' Nest
The Churchill Papers
Murder at Colditz

HELL ON THE RHINE

Duncan Harding

This first world edition published in Great Britain 2003 by
SEVERN HOUSE PUBLISHERS LTD of
9–15 High Street, Sutton, Surrey SM1 1DF.
This first world edition published in the USA 2003 by
SEVERN HOUSE PUBLISHERS INC of
595 Madison Avenue, New York, N.Y. 10022.

British Library Cataloguing in Publication Data

Harding, Duncan, 1926-
    Hell on the Rhine. - (X-craft series)
    1. World War, 1929-1945 - Campaigns - Germany -
        Remagen - Fiction
    2. Ludendorff Bridge (Remagen, Germany) - Fiction
    I. Title
    823.9'14 [F]

    ISBN 0-7278-5886-6

Typeset by Palimpsest Book Production Ltd.,
Polmont, Stirlingshire, Scotland.
Printed and bound in Great Britain by
MPG Books Ltd., Bodmin, Cornwall.

'Over the Rhine, then let us go and finish off the German war as soon as possible . . . And good hunting to you all on the other side!'
Field Marshal Montgomery,
March 23rd, 1945

The Neger

It was the Italians who first made use of 'human torpedoes' in World War II – and with considerable success. Two frogmen sat astride a midget submarine known as a Maiale – 'Pig'; it carried a detachable warhead that they would fasten beneath an enemy ship's keel.

The Germans took the concept a stage further with the Neger – 'Negro', a pun on the surname of its designer, Richard Mohr. The warhead of a G7e torpedo was replaced with a pilot's cockpit and another torpedo was slung below. The pilot started and released the torpedo with a lever. Though it was not intended as a suicide weapon, there were times when the torpedo started but failed to release.

Prelude:

The Black Devil Attack

'Sir, I ain't seen anything like it in twenty years at sea.'
Obermaat Hansen to
Kapitänleutnant Hummel

At a dead slow crawl, its great Maybach engine purring like a huge soft cat, each skimmer, or 'wave rider' as they were known, approached the Russian shallows. To their right, the night sky was stabbed scarlet time and time again, as the Russian flak fired at the raid the *Luftwaffe* was putting in as a feint. The bombing attack was intended to cover any noise the motorboats might make as they came ever closer to Leningrad. It was working, too. They were pretty close to the great Russian naval base's inner harbour – and they still hadn't been spotted.

In the lead craft Kaptänleutnant Hummel, known throughout Germany's Special Forces through a play on his name as 'Bumble Bee', stood very erect, gaze fixed on the green glow of the compass, every nerve in his lean hard body tense with expectation. Hummel wasn't scared. He was simply preparing himself for what he knew was to come: swift bloody action. 'Old hare' that he was, he was prepared for the unexpected, the potential disaster, even though at the moment everything seemed to be going exactly right.

On the shore another stick of 250lb German bombs rippled the length of the sea wall. Everywhere there were sudden violent spurts of flame. For an instant, Hummel could see the line of squat Russian blockhouses silhouetted a stark black against the red glare. 'Try that on for collar size, Ivan!' He meant the Russians. Just like so many lonely men in command he talked to himself when he thought no one was nearby. Hummel thought it did no good to communicate unnecessarily with subordinates; it was always better to keep one's thoughts to oneself.

They were getting close enough now. He bent his white-blond head to the voice tube and as if he believed the Ivans might overhear him, whispered in his hard North German voice, 'Stop engine, Engineer.'

The powerful diesel died to a soft whimper almost at once. To left and right the rest of the little flotilla came to a halt a few moments later. Now they waited there, high-prowed skimmers, which could virtually skim across the surface of the water at forty knots an hour. Now the only sound was that of the air raid over Leningrad and the soft lap-lap of the wavelets against the boats' wooden hulls.

Hummel frowned for some reason known only to himself. The old *Obermaat* in charge of the deck guessed the 'Old Man' (though Hummel was barely twenty-five) was at that moment of decision when, as skipper, he had to decide if the op and the violent lethal action which would surely follow would commence or not. He watched in the red glare from the bombing as Hummel shot another look at the compass and then at the Ivan searchlights weaving wildly to and fro as they searched for the *Luftwaffe* planes swooping to the east prior to coming in for their last sortie.

Then Hummel saw it, reflected in the light of the enemy searchlights. A thick patch of brown on the surface of the water. It was barely there for an instant. Next moment it had vanished. The attack force had reached the shallows. '*Obermaat*,' Hummel hissed sharply.

'*Jawohl. Herr Ka-Lo.*'

'We've reached the shallows . . . drop the buoy.'

The old petty officer didn't hesitate. The longer they waited here, the more likely the Ivans would shove a hot poker up their arses. He issued his own order. The waiting ratings heaved the marker buoy overboard. It dropped with a splash that sounded to a tense Hummel as if it might well be heard from there to Moscow. But already the *Luftwaffe* Junkers 88s were coming in for their last bombing run and the enemy flak had opened up once more. Nobody had heard them. Hummel gave a little sigh of relief. '*Beide Maschinen voraus – langsam!*' he commanded.

The skimmer started up once more. To left and right the others did the same. The V narrowed and the other craft fell into line behind Hummel's command boat. The final phase of the daring attack on Soviet Russia's most powerful and impregnable naval base had begun.

Crawling forward through the dark-brown sluggish water, their ears, eyes and muscles straining, the men of the Black Devils knew if they were discovered now, the Ivans would be able to blow them out of the water with impunity; they wouldn't have a chance. But as Kapitänleutnant Hummel had told them at the briefing, '*Kameraden*, the very boldness of our undertaking will ensure our success. The Ivans won't expect anyone but a man with a little bird that goes tweet-tweet to attempt anything as crazy as this.' He had gazed around at their hard faces with his light-blue eyes and had seen they had appreciated his attempt to lessen their tension with that old kids' phrase for a crazy man. 'Anyway,' he had ended the briefing, 'what can we Black Devils expect – but to die young and make a handsome corpse?' It was then that even the old *Obermaat* had known Hummel had them in the palm of his hand; they'd follow him to hell and back.

Now they were entering that potential hell!

Without warning, a sharp hard white light clicked on to their immediate front. 'Heaven Arse and Cloudburst!' the *Obermaat* cursed to himself. 'That's buggered it!'

Hummel's heart began to beat faster. He felt a nerve begin to tick electrically at the side of his head. He told himself that he had been doing this far too long and that the shit war had been going on for too many years. His nerve was going. Then he remembered Ilse on that terrible morning in Hamburg and told himself yet again what did it all matter? Let his nerve go. Let himself be killed. Even if Germany did manage to still win the war, what did that mean to him? Without Ilse there was nothing to live for, no future, no prospect that whatever he did now, he could ever buy or win happiness for himself. At the back of his mind a harsh little voice rasped abruptly and shook him out of his sudden mood of despair: 'Pull yourself together, you pathetic piss-pansy . . . Just shitting well get on with it!'

He concentrated on that bright white, searching beam. It wavered, as if the searchlight operator had thought he had heard something, but was not too sure whether his ears were playing tricks on him. On the other side of the deck, the old *Obermaat* prayed fervently that the Ivan on the searchlight would think he'd imagined something out to sea and concentrate that threatening beam on the sky once more. All the same, he turned to the young rating manning the twin Spandau machine guns. 'Take aim,' he commanded. 'When I give the word, knock that bastard light out.'

'*Jawohl, Herr Obermaat,*' the kid replied, his voice hoarse with tension. He swung the machine guns round and took aim on that still stationary light. Next moment it moved. It started to approach once more. In a second or two it would pin them down in its merciless light – and then all hell would be let loose.

Suddenly there was a tremendous awe-inspiring crash. The night sky was stabbed by a great dramatic blazing-orange light. The skimmers trembled at the impact. A blast of hot air slammed into Hummel's face. He gasped, as all the air was sucked out of his lungs. Next instant the last wave of bombs began exploding all along the Russian coast. Abruptly the beam went out. Hummel hesitated no longer. 'Drop the next buoy,' he ordered, shouting against the murderous noise of the bombs exploding and the frenzied snap-and-crack of the Russian flak. Over it went and they were moving once more, going in for the kill, every man of the Black Devils sure now that they were going to pull off their daring raid: luck was on their side . . .

As one, the Black Devil squadron fired their flares. It was dangerous, but it had to be done, if the 'Negroes' were going to carry out their death-defying mission with some sort of success. *Plop . . . plop . . . plop!* The flares exploded one after another in bursts of blinding icy-white light. With dramatic suddenness their targets were revealed. Silhouetted a stark black against the white glare there was the Soviet Baltic Fleet. Ship after ship lying in their berths at anchor, like tame sheep in their pens, waiting to be slaughtered.

Now, even as the Russian Aldis lamps started to click their messages of alarm and warning, and the ships' sirens started to screech, the four skimmers surged forward, their 'Negroes' already hanging over their midships waiting to be launched, engines running at the ready.

But that was not yet. Hummel was determined to get in as close as possible and give the dare-devil suicide 'pilots' the best chance possible to make their sacrifice worthwhile.

Like a pack of wild hunting dogs out for the slaughter, scenting blood and prey, the skimmers swept forward, twisting and turning to avoid the fire that their skippers knew would be coming their way soon. Hummel shook his head in silent admiration. What a fine bunch of men –

7

*boy*s, he corrected himself – his Black Devils were. Even at this eleventh hour in Germany's fight to the death, they were still prepared to make the supreme sacrifice for 'Folk, Fatherland and Führer'. Then he forgot his youngsters who only had minutes to live and concentrated on the task at hand.

Now Hummel eased the throttle right back. The prow of the skimmer rose high. A great bow wave curled to left and right in a rush of bubbling white water. Hummel steadied himself with difficulty. The deck trembled beneath his spread feet like a live thing. The skimmer was hitting each wave as if they were brick walls. He felt the blow punch into his lean stomach. Still he kept on relentlessly as red and white tracer began hurrying in his direction like glowing ping-pong balls.

He twisted the controls. The skimmer heeled, twisted and turned crazily. Shells were exploding to left and right in angry spouts of water, splashing down on the craft's deck in sudden deluges. Red hot shards of shells hissed lethally through the rigging. But still the charge continued, the crews of the skimmers carried away by the mad unreasoning lust of battle, sudden death forgotten now in the crazy exhilaration of this atavistic wager with death.

Now the Russian battle fleet, each great ship spouting metal and smoke, seemed a great Goliath, impervious to any blow these puny Davids in their fragile wooden craft could level at it. But the Russians were wrong. They were in for a shocking surprise.

As the Russian gunners recovered their nerve and started returning fire with more deliberate accuracy, the strange shapes that each skimmer was carrying were released into the water. They splashed down and for a few moments were left behind the hurrying skimmers, as if they had been abandoned like some unnecessary weight. Not for long.

With abrupt flurries of agitated white water, the Negroes' motors kicked into action. Suddenly all eight of them were catching up with the skimmers, which would soon break off their attack, as soon as Hummel judged the new secret weapons were on course and that there might be a chance of picking up their pilots.

Now the Soviet fire was ripping into Hummel's skimmer. The radio mast went, tumbling down in a flurry of angry violet sparks. In front of him the bridge's protective glass shattered into a crazy spider's web. To his port one of the skimmers had been more seriously hit. Thick black oily smoke was pouring from its engine room and she was beginning to lose speed. Hummel knew instinctively, his luck was beginning to run out. It was time to break off the skimmers' part of the attack before it was too late. He yelled above the ear-splitting roar of the Maybach engines going on all out. '*Obermaat . . . Aktion abbrechen!*'

'Ay ay, sir . . . break off action!' the old sailor repeated.

In a great roaring sweep, Hummel swung his skimmer round. In that same instant he reduced speed. The skimmer's knife-like prow dropped and the white curling wave ceased. It was a dangerous manoeuvre. But Hummel knew it was one he had to make. For perhaps two to three minutes, he would be a sitting duck for the Soviet gunners, who now had his range and at this decidedly reduced speed had a good chance of blowing the skimmer out of the water.

Forcing himself to keep calm, Hummel began counting off the seconds in tens. He reached one minute. On all sides shells were falling. Great gushes of water seemed about to sink the skimmer time and time again. The craft was buffeted crazily from side to side, as if punched by a mighty invisible fist. Doggedly he kept on counting.

'*Forty . . . fifty . . .*' He told himself that the pilots would have released their torpedoes (if they had survived this far). '*Sixty . . . seven—*' His count was interrupted by a clear clang of steel striking steel. A sheet of scarlet flame rent the night sky apart. 'Holy strawsack!' the old *Obermaat* yelled, blinded by the glare. '*Ich werde verruckt—*' The rest of his words were drowned by the great roar of a ship's boilers bursting. Hummel flew a hurried glance over his shoulder. The nearest Soviet cruiser had exploded. The Negro had hit its target. Her back arched upwards. The masts came tumbling down. Smoke started to gush from every hole. Metal debris shot hundreds of metres into a sky that had become as bright as day.

'*EIN VOLLTREFFER!*' the little *Obermaat* shouted joyfully, jumping up and down like an excited schoolkid. 'A hit . . . *a real hit!*'

'Look out for the pilots,' Hummel yelled back, trying to throw cold water on the little petty officer's understandable joy at their triumph. 'The poor swine need all the help they can get if they've survived.'

'*Klar, Herr Ka-Lo,*' the petty officer answered, immediately brought down to earth again in the same instant that another Soviet warship was hit and to port an enemy cruiser exploded with a great flame searing its upper deck like a giant blowtorch. She started to keel over. The violent flame ripped the length of the hull. Her buckled plates caught fire. Their grey paint began to bubble and writhe, as if it had an independent life of its own. Everywhere screaming enemy sailors, some of them already flaming torches, tried to dive for it. To no avail.

As they scrambled and slid down the hull trying to find a place to divè from, explosion after explosion began ripping her apart. Then with frightening, appalling suddenness, the cruiser sank beneath the water with a great shriek of escaping steam. A moment later there was nothing of her to be seen, save the debris and dead floating in the water, which was exploding in obscene bubbles of escaping air like gross giant farts.

The little *Obermaat* crossed himself abruptly and breathed in an awed voice: 'Did you see that, sir? . . . I ain't seen nothing like that in twenty years at sea. *Himmelherrje, was ein Theater!*'

Hummel didn't react. He was concentrating on two things now: getting his skimmers out safely and picking up any of the pilots who had survived the suicidal attack, and then tucking his hind legs under his arms and running like hell before the Ivans sent out their dive-bombers.

For now the enemy was really reacting. The Ivans had recovered from their initial shock. Every ship, trapped as the Baltic Fleet was in its anchorage, had opened up from her berth. Now the sky was criss-crossed with the lethal morse of red, green and white tracer. Already those closest to the attackers were lowering fast launches, their crews, half dressed, tumbling into them, only too eager to get to grips with these insolent, if daredevil attackers. On the mole, staff cars were racing back and forth, fully lit, and Hummel could guess they could only contain officers hurrying to headquarters to order an instant blockage of the Baltic narrows in an attempt to stop the 'Fritzes' escaping to their own bases in Konigsberg, Stettin and the like.

Hummel flashed a glance at the green-glowing dial of his wristwatch. He guessed there was only one Negro left which hadn't carried out its attack. He'd give the unknown pilot two minutes to do so. Then he'd have picked up any survivors and would be on his way westwards before the Ivans—

He didn't think the thought to its conclusion. As a Soviet oil tanker was hit and a great searing purple flame shot hundreds of metres into the sky and there was that grating frightening sound of metal being torn apart, the skimmer to his immediate starboard was abruptly blinded by two searchlights interlinked and pinning it down in a bright cone of white light. The Soviets didn't waste time. Desperately the young skipper threw his craft from side to side in great combs of wild white water. To no avail.

Then it happened. Even as the Soviet guns homed in on the trapped speedboat, the skimmer ran straight into its neighbour, Skimmer Number Three, at an acute angle. 'Oh for God's sake – *no!*' Hummel cried in despair.

But the skipper of the first skimmer kept his head. Outlined clearly in the light of the Soviet searchlights, he signalled the other skipper to stop engines. He obeyed instantly, leaving his fate in the hands of his comrade. Hummel licked suddenly parched lips. He guessed what the first skipper was going to attempt to do. He hoped he would.

Opening his throttle the widest it would go, the Maybach engines screaming in protest at the strain, the skimmer's propellers thrashing the water at her stern into a crazy fury, he backed off, taking the trapped skimmer with him. Thus in this strange locked position like two insects stuck together in the midst of copulation, the first craft dragged the other one with it.

Hummel felt the cold sweat trickle down the small of his back. His fists were clenched. His nails dug into the palms of his hands cruelly and painfully, as he willed the crazy manoeuvre to succeed.

But the Ivans were not going to be cheated of their prey. Now it seemed that every gun in the burning fleet concentrated its fire on the hopelessly slow skimmers. Tracer raced towards them furiously. The sea around the two craft was lashed with spent bullets and shrapnel. Red electric ripples ran the length of the skimmers' decks, as the enemy machine guns peppered their superstructure. Woodwork splintered like matchwood. Masts came tumbling down. Machine-gun crews fell dead at their guns, firing still even in death.

Hummel forgot the surviving pilots wherever they might be. He concentrated on the trapped skimmers. Fervently he prayed like he had never prayed before that they might succeed in reaching the cover of the outer sea wall, which would provide some protection for the already shattered craft and where he might be able to take the survivors aboard and escape.

But that wasn't to be. As yet another Soviet ship exploded, proving that all the pilots had done their job well, there was a huge boom. Great 120mm shells howled above Hummel's craft like the sound of a midnight express hurtling through an empty station. They landed – Hummel couldn't see exactly where – but when the great mass of smoke had disappeared, the two skimmers had vanished from the face of the sea. Behind they left a few planks tossing in the wild water and what looked like half a body kept afloat by a yellow life jacket. Otherwise nothing.

In the loud echoing silence that followed, Hummel raised his hand to his cap in a kind of sad salute: a salute to all the brave young men who had died for Folk, Fatherland and Führer – and what he knew in his heart was a hopeless cause. He turned (and later the old *Obermaat* would swear to his cronies of the petty officers' mess, 'you know the Old Man had tears in his eyes – he's a hard bastard, as you lot know, but tears there were, of that I'm sure') and rapped out his orders.

The surviving skimmers turned and hurried back into the Baltic, heading west at top speed. The Black Devils had won their last victory this May day of 1944. From now onwards it would be defeat after defeat . . .

Harding:

'The Most Famous Bridge in the World – for a Week!'

I 've never gone much on the Jerries.
     That may surprise you, gentle reader, to hear that. As all of you know by now, normally I'm brimming over with the milk of human kindness and love for the whole world and its citizens. But the Jerries . . . I just don't know.

Sometimes when I consider the matter, which isn't often (I mean, who in his right mind today is really interested in the Germans?), I think it might be something to do with my 'Old Dad' and the 'War'. After all, as soon as he realized he had got Mum in the family way in 1939, he bravely volunteered for the British Army straight off. He was like that, my Old Dad. Took the 'King's Shilling', as they called it in those great days of yore, and off he went to do his duty for the King-Emperor. He told Mum he didn't want to go, especially now as she had a bun in the oven, but Britain needed him. My Old Dad seems to have been like that – very decent and a real patriot.

We never saw him again, something for which I blame the Jerries even today, I suppose. As I heard it later in the orphange (my Mum had to put me in it after the nasty business with the Yank master sergeant), he had been posted missing, believed killed in action at Dunkirk. A hero's death would have been typical of my Old Dad.

A few years back when I made some enquiries at the Ministry of Defence (I thought there might have been some entitlement to a pension or a lump sum maybe) the tart at Records told me he was still posted, after all that time, as 'missing'. According to her it had not happened at Dunkirk but Catterick, some place in the wilds of North Yorkshire when he'd done a bunk from the 'Shit and Shovel Brigade', the Pioneer Corps to you, dear reader.

But you know these toffee-nosed clerks, they're still the same after all that time under our noble leader Mr B. Thick and stand-offish. Fancy suggesting that my brave Old Dad had gone on the trot because he'd put the old woman up the spout! A diabolical liberty. I wrote to that old boozer of an MP of mine about it. Whatever . . . Anyhow, what caused it, I just don't know, but I simply do not like Jerries!

So it came as a bit of a surprise (and yours truly can't get very surprised these days – they'd have to put me up for the Booker to get a gasp out of this old hack) when my publisher made the almost unbelievable suggestion that I should go to Krautland – me visit the Third Reich?! Took my very breath away, I can tell you. Nearly choked on the goulash that we were eating at the time. He who must be obeyed, my publisher, doesn't half like foreign grub.

He said he'd heard a tremendous story. 'Right up your street, Duncan. Easy for you to turn into one of your celebrated novels. If you agree to tackle the project, I'd like you to have a look-see at the sites of the real action etc. – all expenses paid.'

I nearly flipped my lid, but he said the magic words without batting an eyelid and took another swallow of that red 'Mouton' stuff he drinks that costs fifty quid just to look at the label on the bottle.

'All expenses paid!' I couldn't help but exclaim. What had gone wrong with him? Was it the booze? Or had he really come across a good true life story that could be turned into one of my 'celebrated novels'? I mean, I'd

always thought he'd rather eat his own children than spend money on his authors, celebrated or otherwise.

In a way I was right. In the event 'all expenses paid' turned out to be Stansted and that Mick airline, where you stand all the way to your destination and a sandwich from the stewardess's trolley costs more than a flight by Concorde. But that's another tale.

The story, according to my publisher, concerned 'the most famous bridge in the world – *for a week*!' The bridge in question had been located on the German Rhine River at an obscure little place called Remagen. Apparently in March '45, this bridge had been the only one left standing across the great Kraut river. Naturally all the top Allied brass were lusting after it all those years ago. First general across and he'd gain the kudos of victory: the guy who gave Old Adolf's Third Reich the final knock on the noddle.

Naturally, according to my publisher, who by now was in fine form, well into his second bottle of this 'Mouton' stuff, the Allies captured this bridge at Remagen. But Old Adolf wasn't going to let them get away with it. He hatched all sorts of weird and wonderful counter-offensive plans. One included the use of Negroes.

'I beg your pardon?'

He tried to tell me what they were, but I could see he wasn't too clued up on the subject and anyway at that stage of the deal I wasn't particularly interested. Old hacks like yours truly might not be in the Nobel Prize for Literature category, but we do know how to make up the 'facts'. Get me to the nearest public library with a couple of stiff whiskys beneath my belt and I'd be the world expert on those 'Negroes' of his in zero, comma, nothing seconds!

Besides at that moment my mind was concentrating on that 'all expenses paid' bit. Normally I spend a lot my 'advance' – that's the meagre money bait that publishers give to their hacks to sucker them into writing their 'celebrated novels' – in doing the necessary research before I begin to write. Now here his nibs was drinking his 'Mouton' and scoffing his foreign Hungarian goulash and actually offering me the dibs *extra*! It was enough to bring tears to my poor old eyes.

It was as if the Good Lord sitting up there on his fleecy-white cloud had just placed his gentle hand on 'Dunc's' fevered brow and soothed all cares away. For indeed, dear reader, as you can imagine, my mind had been racing with vivid pictures of what the immediate future might now hold for me.

Why, with 'all expenses paid' – those magic words – there might even be some lusty blonde Gretchen, with breasts like silken pillows, a chambermaid in some olde worlde Kraut hostellerie perhaps, who'd give a generous Dunc a swift whirl beneath the *Federdecke* ('duvet,' to you, gentle reader).

So, despite my doubts about the Huns, I accepted my publisher's offer with unaccustomed alacrity. For I must confess, I thought once the effect of the 'Mouton' had worn off, he might have second thoughts about 'all expenses paid'. God knows what I was supposed to find at this place, Remagen. But that didn't matter. What I couldn't find, as I've said before, I could make up. Thus it was a cognac, a 'gentleman's handshake' of agreement, a cheque back in the office (yes, a cheque *there and then*; none of that old 'cheque's in the post' lark) and a day later I was standing in one of those Mick aeroplanes crossing the Channel and heading for darkest Krautland . . .

Book One:

Die Wacht am Rhein*

'We're gonna have a party on the Rhine.'
Dwight D. Eisenhower,
Allied Supreme Commander,
March 1946

* Watch on the Rhine.

One

March 2nd, 1945

In the distance the heavy guns continued to rumble. Over the Rhine, the night sky flickered pink as the German counter-barrage tried to stop the advancing Americans. But the Americans were not going to be stopped. For this night 'Big Simp', as the shaven-headed commander of the US 9th Army was known to his men, had ordered, cost what it may, they would capture one or both of two remaining bridges across Germany's greatest natural barrier. For this night, his leading elements had just reported that to north and south of the Rhenish city of Düsseldorf there were two bridges that, with a bit of luck, they might rush and capture by daybreak.

Now Big Simp had given his men the green light to attack and seize the bridge located in the suburb of Oberkassel. There was one catch, however. The bridge was located in a densely populated industrial area, where his men might have to fight for every house, even if they were only defended, as Big Simp put it, by 'some old prick of a Home Guard and his kid in Hitler Youth pants'. That would mean the Germans could blow up the vital bridge whenever they felt the need to do so. 'The Joes'll have to trick the Krauts and get close enough to rush the goddam bridge,' Big Simp had told his chief of staff, 'so that they don't have any time to blow her up . . . Kind of Trojan Horse tactics.'

23

Now as the guns thundered and the tense German defenders waited for what was to come, the volunteers for the attack, all of them German-speakers, were doing exactly that. They were going to attempt to fool the Krauts into believing they were a German outfit retreating from the chaotic lost battle of the Rhine back to their own lines. All of them knew that if they were captured by the enemy, dressed as they now were in captured German uniforms complete with coal-scuttle helmets, the Germans would be entitled to shoot them out of hand as spies. But it was a risk that Big Simp was prepared to take. As he had personally told the assault force's battalion commander an hour before, 'Get me that bridge, Colonel, and I'll give you and your whole battalion a three-day pass in Gay Paree. . . . Pig Alley'll be all yours and I don't even give a goddam if some if your Joes come back with a little *souvenir d'amour*,' * and the Army Commander had actually winked at the younger officer.

While the assault infantry prepared for their bold action, the tankers who would carry them to the bridge on their tanks camouflaged their vehicles to make them look like German panzers. They cut down ammunition tubes and taped them to their cannon to make them more like the typical German tank cannon. They painted large white identification numbers on their turrets in the German fashion and transformed the distinctive US radio aerials – a dead giveaway to any German defender that this was an American tank – into a German-style rod aerial.

Now in complete darkness, broken only by the sudden flashes of shells exploding, the bold little force rumbled

* 'Pig Alley' was the GIs' name for Paris's Place Pigalle, the base for the capital's whores.

down the main road leading to the bridge at Oberkassel. In the column, the only noise was the soft rumble of the Shermans' rubber tracks. For the battalion commander had ordered: no talking, no smoking. For he reasoned that the Germans, reduced to smoking only their home-grown evil-smelling weed, would recognize the perfumed smell of a Camel or Lucky immediately.

Luck, it seemed, was on their side. They passed the first German strongpoint without even being challenged. A little later they ran into what looked like a whole company of German infantry. The disguised GIs crowded on the decks of the tanks tensed. A few reached for their rifles. Were the Krauts going to make a fight of it? They weren't. The Americans' disguise fooled the enemy. Obediently the column of infantry got out of their way and stood at the side of the road to let the armour rumble past. As one GI breathed to his neighbour, 'Jesus, I nearly pissed myself!' 'What d'ya mean *nearly*?' the other GI snarled in a hoarse whisper. 'I've got piss dribbling all down my goddam right leg!'

By three hours after they had started out, the Trojan Horse column had reached Oberkassel, well behind German lines, and were passing into the industrial suburb without having fired a single shot. Big Simp's bold attempt to take the vital bridge across the Rhine by a *coup de main* seemingly was paying off. One of two Rhine bridges in the whole of the US 9th Army's sector was now within reach.

To the east, the first ugly white light of the new dawn was beginning to lighten the sky. Everything was outlined a stark black. For now the barrage had ceased, as if the German defenders felt safe for the time being and were saving ammunition for the day when the real attack on the Rhine would commence. Indeed it seemed to the tense,

25

disguised US troopers that the whole front had gone back to sleep. The cobbled approach to the bridge was apparently empty. Not a defender in sight.

Now, however, things began to go wrong. Abruptly, seemingly out of nowhere, a lone German soldier appeared, riding a battered old bicycle. He started to pedal by the slow-moving column. At first he showed no interest. Suddenly, however, those closest to the lone German noted a look of suspicion in his face. He had spotted something wrong. For a moment the battalion commander's hand fell to his pistol. Should he attempt to shoot the German? If he did, would that sound the alarm? He hesitated. Just a moment or two too long. Suddenly, as he cleared the tail of the tank column, the cyclist bent his head over his handlebars. The battalion commander shouted. To no avail.

Now the German was pedalling all out. 'He's spotted us!' someone yelled. On the deck of the rear tank, a GI raised his German rifle and took swift aim. His rifle cracked off a single shot. The German cried with pain. His cycle wobbled. Next moment the German fell out of the saddle and tumbled to the cobbles, dead before he hit them.

Now things began to move – fast. Over near the Rhine, the air-raid sirens started to shriek an instant warning. 'Roll 'em!' the battalion commander yelled into the deck mike. Below him the tank driver put his foot down. The Sherman shot forward. Behind it the rest of the column quickened speed, too. In one last desperate attempt, the GI column raced for the bridge. But now the German defenders were reacting. Scarlet flame stabbed the dawn greyness. Kids with primitive German missile launchers ran into the road, fired and ducked, as a rocket sped towards the hurrying tanks like an angry red hornet. Here and there a tank was hit, scattering the GIs on deck on to the road, where those who survived started returning the enemy fire.

The lead tank swung round the last corner. From a bomb-shattered building there, the Germans began tossing stick grenades on the tank. It continued at full speed, ignoring the grenades exploding on both sides of it like bombs! Holy mackerel!' the commander yelled. 'There she is!'

It was the bridge and it was still intact!

'Give her all ya've got,' the commander cried above the angry snap-and-crack of the fire fight. The sweating driver in his leather helmet did so, trying to ignore the whine of the shrapnel howling off the tank's metal hull and praying that no little Hitler Youth bastard, eager for glory and early death, would spring out of the trenches on both sides of the approach road and fire at him with his *Panzerfaust* rocket launcher.

The tank driver need not have feared. For in that very same instant, the bridge ahead – so close and yet so far – appeared to tremble. On it, German engineers were springing out of culverts and running all out for the far end, as if the Devil himself were after them.

'Hot shit – *NO!*' the battalion commander groaned and slapped his hand to his head in despair. For now a series of angry blue sparks was running the length of the bridge and he knew what that signified. The Krauts were beginning to blow it.

Now the girders were trembling. A low angry rumbling was beginning to grow. Here and there puffs of grey smoke rose from the road. The trembling grew more violent. Suddenly, startlingly, the centre of the bridge disintegrated in an angry ball of red and sickly-yellow flame. A huge mushroom of smoke raced for the sky. As the tank commander reeled back, gasping for breath, deafened totally, what was left of the bridge across the Rhine River slithered and splashed into the water. Big Simp's first attempt to capture a bridge over Nazi Germany's last major natural bulwark had failed miserably . . .

The second attempt was made that very same day. This time no subterfuge would be employed. Big Simp's Second Armored Division, the 'Hell on Wheels' as the American division liked to call itself, would go all out for the 'Adolf Hitler Brücke, stretching 1,640 feet across the Rhine at nearby Uerdingen.

Confident and cocky, as the Second always was, the men believed what their divisional commander told them. They were going to head straight for the last remaining bridge on the 9th Army front and take it by force. 'It would be a sock in the eye for Adolf.' Unfortunately, as bold as the Second was, it would be unable to deliver that particular punch to Adolf's optic.

Within minutes of the Second launching its attack at midday, it had lost four Shermans, knocked out by German anti-tank guns. Hastily infantry were whistled to try to clean up the mess. They didn't. But the hard-pressed GIs fighting from street corner to corner, blasting away at every upper storey where they suspected German snipers or tossing in grenades at every cellar opening, did manage to start pushing the defenders back – and there was still no report that the enemy was attempting to blow up the one remaining bridge.

By four the men of the 'Hell on Wheels' were still confident they could take the bridge and their commanding general ordered his artillery to begin laying down harassing fire on the entrance to the bridge itself. It might pothole the approach road, but he reasoned that it would keep the Kraut engineers' heads down and prevent them activating their explosive charges. Every thirty seconds, the general commanded his gunners to drop a medium-sized shell at both ends of the bridge.

The tactic seemed to work. When darkness fell, the bridge was still intact and HQ was already working out a plan to take the bridge before many hours had passed. Indeed they were requesting Big Simp's headquarters for a paradrop on the bridge itself to ensure that this time they didn't lose it at the last minute.

But abruptly that no longer seemed necessary. A signal flashed to the 'Hell on Wheels' HQ that a young tank lieutenant and his troop of tanks had actually already crossed to the other side. Unfortunately the young officer had no sense of history. The fact that he was the first American to cross the Rhine in combat during World War Two didn't seem to interest him. Instead of staying where he was, he hurried back to the American side. It was a fateful oversight. Now the Germans made a last determined attempt to stop the bridge falling into the hands of the *Amis*.

While the Second Armored Division readied two battalions of infantry to cross, the German engineers crept out of their explosives chambers and foxholes and prepared to destroy the bridge.

Now the 1,000 or so infantrymen moved forward, crouched low, walking slowly and steadily like countrymen crossing a field in heavy pelting rain. One battalion of them was to secure the far end; the other, the end on the American side. Thus they would hold the whole length of the structure while US engineers searched it for demolition charges.

Everything went according to plan. Indeed the leading elements of the infantry had actually crossed and penetrated a hundred yards into German-held territory when they made a frightening discovery: the roadbed there wouldn't support tanks. That did it. The infantrymen reasoned, if they *were* cut off in the middle of 'Krautland' without armour, they'd be dead ducks.

Discipline went out of the window. They broke. Despite the pleas and threats of their officers, they left their positions and formations and pelted back to the US side of the great river. It wasn't a retreat; it was a panic-stricken rout.

But perhaps the frightened infantrymen were right to act as they did when they did. For the German engineers didn't need a second invitation to destroy the Adolf Hitler Brücke now that the *Amis* had panicked and made a run for it. Hastily they started to replace the demolition charges which the enemy had destroyed as they had crossed the bridge. Even as the American commanders started to regroup their troops and reorganize them for another crossing of the Rhine, there was an ear-splitting explosion. A moment later it was followed by another – and yet another.

On the western bank, the re-formed infantrymen of the 'Hell on Wheels' stood open-mouthed in awe at the great spectacle, the blast buffeting their faces like a blow from a flabby damp fist. Now the eastern half of the structure was swaying and trembling crazily, dust and smoke spiralling into the leaden sky. A moment later, though it seemed an eternity to those watching, the Adolf Hitler Brücke thundered and slithered into the water below.

Big Simp's hopes of capturing a bridge over the Rhine and beating Field Marshal Sir Bernard Law Montgomery across had been dashed. Now the tall American Army commander with his sharp profile and polished bald head – he looked like some marauding eighteenth-century Mohawk Indian – would have to wait until the little Britisher with his holier-than-thou manner allowed him to cross . . .

It was later that day that the Second Armored Division's senior Intelligence officer made his strange discovery.

He was accompanied by Tech. Sergeant Levisohn, his interpreter who had been born not more than twenty miles from where the Major and he now combed the German dead sprawled everywhere along the banks of the American-held side of the Rhine. It was the custom and self-imposed unpleasant duty of the two of them to check enemy bodies after any battle in the search for information that might be of some use. They were looking for unit identifications, paybooks, insignia and the like – anything that might help to build up the intricate mosaic of the intelligence 'big picture'.

As always the battlefield was an ugly place: the dead sprawled out in heaps in the wild abandoned postures of those done to death violently; the customary victims of a shelling, their guts torn open, intestines nestled in the bloody hole like coiled grey snakes; and the mournful blacks of the Graves Registration Outfits in their long glistening slickers, all rolling eyes and southern 'mush-mouthed' exclamations of horror.

But the Major and his Sergeant were used to such things now. They carried out their routine duties searching the dead, turning them over with the toes of their boots, as if the dead were afflicted by some terrible contagious disease (which they were – namely, death), groping inside the dead Germans' tunics to find their *Soldbuchs*, checking their metal ID discs. It was about halfway through their search, as on the German side of the Rhine, a multiple mortar opened up and began loosing its screaming, frightening great shells at the blacks loading the 'stiffs' into the 'meatwagon', that they came across a dead German wearing a uniform that they didn't encounter very often.

It was a man dressed in the dark blue of the *Kriegsmarine*, the German Navy. He lay on his back, his face unblemished and young, eyes wide open, staring at the grey sky above.

Both his legs had been shot off at the knee and the Major guessed he had died slowly to judge from the pool of sticky black blood in which he lay. 'Funny, Sergeant, a sailor here,' he commented almost to himself.

Levisohn was, as always, quick on the uptake, that's why the Major employed him, though he didn't particularly like Jews, especially German ones: 'The Rhine, sir,' he said in his accented English. 'The Krauts'll have naval patrols on it.'

'Sure, I guess you're right,' the Major answered. 'But look at the size of that stiff's upper thigh muscles.' He indicated where the trousers had been torn away by the shell. Above the knees the dead sailor's muscles rippled powerfully beneath the still flesh. 'He looks like those guys we saw in the '36 Olympics.' He sighed. 'Poor guy, I guess he'll be doing no more running.'

In that Continental fashion of his, the Sergeant cocked his head to one side, as if to indicate to his superior that he was thinking about the problem occasioned by the dead sailor's leg muscles. Suddenly his dark face lit up. 'Look at the patch on his shoulder, sir,' he exclaimed, the muscles forgotten immediately. 'We've never seen one like that before, have we, sir?'

Behind his gold-rimmed glasses, the Major's eyes narrowed and he stared at what he took to be some sort of unit insignia sewn on to the right shoulder of the dead man's reefer jacket. Mostly Germans belonging to special formations like the SS or Paratroops had an armband with the name of their outfit imprinted on it. This insignia was totally different. It depicted what looked like a Satan type of figure riding a sausage-like object, which could have been a torpedo, through the waves. Below picked out in gold and black were the words '*Die Schwarzen Teufel*'. The Major looked at the Sergeant.

Levisohn thought: What an idiot! He's a senior Intelligence officer and can't even speak the enemy's language. *Meschugge!* Aloud, he said in his normal very polite fashion, 'It means the "Black Devils", sir.'

The Major pondered the title for a few moments. On the other side of the Rhine, the enemy was increasing the mortar barrage and the blacks in the line of fire had already dropped the mattress covers which served as body bags for the American dead and taken shelter behind a couple of knocked-out Sherman tanks. After a time, he said, 'What do you make of it, Sergeant?'

Levisohn could have made out a lot of things, but he had soon learned when he had volunteered for the US Army back in '42 that in the world's most democratic state 'rank hath its privileges'. Whatever he suggested, the Major would later make out any suggestion he made had been his own idea. So he contented himself with: 'Looks like the insignia of some special outfit, sir. Man on a torpedo, sir.'

'But what the Sam Hill is some navy special outfit doing here, riding goddam torpedoes, I ask ya?!'

Sergeant Levisohn had no answer for that particular question and he remained silent as another trident of smoke shot upwards into the sky, heralding a new barrage of bombs. The Major cringed and cried, 'That goddam noise. Why do the Krauts have to have such fucking noisy mortars?' He didn't wait for an answer. Instead he snapped sharply, 'OK, cut the insignia off, Sergeant. We'll take it back with us to Div. HQ. I'm goddam well going to get those coloured boys moving . . . hiding behind the tanks like that.' Next moment he was running with surprising speed for a man of his age and bulk for the protection of the shot-up Shermans' armour.

Levisohn shook his head as if in sorrow at the state of

the world this March morning, then he pulled out his knife and began carrying out the Major's command. Next to him the dead sailor stared sightlessly with bright blue eyes at the sky, his gaze revealing nothing save, perhaps, the futility of it all.

Two

'*Morgen, Herr Generalfeldmarschall*,' the staff officers in their elegant tunics, with the purple stripe
of the Greater General Staff running down their riding
breeches, barked. As one they clicked their highly polished
boots together in the position of attention. Powerful men as
they were, in charge of the destinies of thousands of German soldiers on the western bank of the Rhine, they were
obviously scared of the little officer who marched briskly
into the entrance hall of the medieval castle, which served
as 15th Army's HQ, already tugging off his greatcoat
and handing it to the harassed orderly, who was trailing
red-faced behind him, picking up cap, stick, revolver belt
and now greatcoat.

Field Marshal Model, known as the 'Führer's Fire
Brigade', screwed his monocle more firmly in his eye,
momentarily inspected the high-ranking staff officers, as
if they were a bunch of raw recruits, then snapped crisply,
'*Morgen, meine Herren*.' Then, raising his harsh North
German voice, he demanded, 'Well then, don't stand
around. There's a war to be won. *Where's the damned
fire?*' The man who had saved the Eastern Front four
times and had lately beaten the British at Arnhem, was
living up to his reputation of being the only German
general capable of the role of the 'Führer's Fireman'.

A minute later he was being ushered nervously into the

35

presence of General von Zangen, the tall, square-jawed commander of the 15th Army, who was holding this forty-kilometre section of the Rhine for him. Again Model wasted no time. He strode to the big map of the area on the wall behind von Zangen's desk, slapped it and proclaimed, 'You must be mad, General!'

Von Zangen flushed hotly. 'W-what . . . How do you mean, Field Marshal?' he stuttered unhappily. He knew Model of old. He was admired by the 'old hares' of the frontline, but hated like poison by his commanders and senior staff officers.

'How do I mean?' Model snapped sarcastically, as if he were talking to an idiot. 'I'll tell you. You want to withdraw troops and back up the Rhine defences. You know what that would mean? Those damned stubble-hoppers of yours, once they started moving back, they'd never stop. You'd find the swine heading for Hamburg and the North Sea before you could stop them running. How can you justify such a drastic relocation of troops like that?'

Von Zangen tried. He attempted not to lose his temper and said as calmly as he could, 'As you know, sir, Napoleon once said, "He who tries to defend everything, ends up defending nothing." Any day now, sir, the American Hodges' First Army will try to slip by my flank as I am positioned now and send their armour shooting for the Rhine – say around Remagen.' He tapped the map.

'What nonsense!' Model cut him off. 'We've seen the *Amis* have failed at Düsseldorf, where if they had captured the bridges, they would have been straight on to the autobahn net.' Now he *slapped* the map, his notoriously bad temper flaring up. 'Only a fool would attempt to cross the Rhine at Remagen, where the cliffs rise steeply from the eastern bank and where the road network is little more than tracks.' He paused and gasped for breath. 'What could that do for them? The Americans are fools admittedly, but not such great boobies. They will cross in the north where Montgomery is – and thank God, that particular British field marshal is very slow . . .' He smirked suddenly, as if he was thinking of the contrast between his own hurried tactics and those of the little Englishman. 'Remagen is not important for the *Amis*.' He dismissed the matter with a contemptuous wave of his hand . . .

Model would have been surprised if he had known that at that particular moment, an obscure American commander, General Hoge of the US Ninth Armored Division, was discussing that self-same Rhenish town and its bridge, the railway bridge across the Rhine at Remagen.

He had just walked into his headquarters some twenty miles away from Remagen to find his bespectacled division commander, General Leonard, peering at his situation map through a magnifying glass.

'How's it going?' Leonard asked, straightening up with a little groan of middle-age stiffness.

'Not bad,' Hoge said and, not a man given to idle small talk, he walked right over to the map that his divisional commander had just been studying. He pointed to the centre of the rash of blue and red crayon marks which marked the units holding the German front and the US ones advancing on them. 'How about this bridge across the river?' he said, drawing a circle in red around the German town.

'What about it?'

'Intelligence can't tell whether the bridge there has been blown or not. Suppose my guys find it hasn't, should I take it?'

As if it was customary that divisional generals should make decisions that might affect the whole balance of the

37

American campaign in Europe, Leonard answered easily, 'Hell, yes. Go and get it.'

Just at that moment the Divisional Commander noticed one of his staff officers was beginning to buckle on his pistol. 'Where the hell do you think you're going?' he demanded in surprise.

'Well, if the outfit near Remagen is going to take that bridge there, I guess I'd better go and tell their commanding officer.' He grinned. 'We're too close to the Krauts to put the order on the horn.' He meant the field telephone.

Now it was Leonard's turn to grin. 'Yeah, I guess you're right. Go up there and maybe you'll get your name in the papers.'

The staff officer was suddenly serious. 'General,' he said, 'I don't want my name in the papers.' He grabbed his helmet. 'I just want to finish this war and damn well go home.'

Thus it was that three obscure staff officers decided the fate of the campaign in Europe. Without any checking with their army headquarters, while at Montgomery's 2nd Army HQ a massive crossing of the Rhine was being planned to involve two parachute divisions, commandos, thousands of planes, whole corps of infantry divisions, three American officers were now about to set the wheels in motion which would make the bridge at Remagen, for a while, *'the most famous bridge in the world . . .'*

Just after one that day, the leading task force of the Ninth Armored Division reached a section of the woods directly above Remagen. The young officer in charge slipped through the trees carefully, holding his carbine at the ready and thought he'd be first in his outfit to see the Rhine. The Ninth had been fighting in Europe for four long bloody months now and he had been in the thick of it. He felt he deserved a first look at the river which now barred the way to the final destruction of the Third Reich. But as he came out of the trees, carefully keeping low, finger on the trigger of his carbine, he saw more than he had bargained for.

There below, there was not only the Rhine. South of Remagen was a great railway bridge, with planks fixed over the tracks so that trucks and other light vehicles could use it; and vehicles were using it at this very moment, passing from west to east. The bridge was still intact and that young officer would remember to the day he would die that he had been the first soldier in the Allied armies to catch the first glimpse of 1,000-foot-long Ludendorff Bridge, now to be the most famous bridge in the world.

He whistled softly. As far as he could see, the Krauts were making no attempt to defend the place. Instead they were streaming across to the eastern side in what seemed to him panic. 'Jesus H. Christ!' he whispered to himself. 'The whole goddam shoot is there for the taking.' Suddenly the young officer became aware of the magnitude of his discovery. Hell, he had to act. He had to report this back to the company and then up channels toot sweet. Somebody was going to have to capture that bridge down there before the Krauts blew it and as he crawled back into the trees of the heights, he told himself he knew already who that was going to be. As usual it would be the 'P.B.I.' – the poor bloody infantry – *the poor bloody infantry . . . !*

But the Germans on the bridge were already aware that trouble was coming their way. That morning, disobeying Model's decision that the bridge was in no danger, von Zangen had sent one of his own staff officers, Major Hans Scheller, to take command. He was to defend the bridge to the last moment so that von Zangen's retreating 15th Army could get across, but as soon as the *Amis* were in sight and looked as if they were going to make a crossing, he was to order Captain Friesenheim, the engineer officer in charge of demolitions, to blow the Ludendorff Railway Bridge immediately – and Scheller was going to carry out those orders to the letter. For he already knew, if he failed to do so, the Führer would demand his head. Failure would mean his summary execution.

Indeed Scheller was so worried about failure and the inevitable punishment that would follow that he decided the bridge would be blown within the next few hours, before the *Amis* appeared, and to make sure that the authorities would know afterwards, he started dictating the order he was about to give to a soldier clerk.

Standing at the entrance to the railway on the far side of the bank, Captain Friesenheim, the tall craggy engineer officer, listened as the staff officer from Corps relayed the order. At the same time he eyed the western bank. There everything was in total confusion. Soldiers and civilians were inextricably mixed. Military vehicles packed with weary ragged infantry were trying to force their way through the scared civilians, dragging behind them their pathetic possessions in wooden carts. Others had unearthed cars powered by gas bags on their roofs and camouflaged by hastily plucked greenery; they were hooting their horns and threatening to run down everything and anything that got in the path of their panic-stricken flight to the tunnel on the eastern bank of the great railway bridge. As for the 'chaindogs', the military policemen, who were supposed to be regulating this crazy stream of fleeing military and civilians across the Rhine, they had given up the task. As Friesenheim watched them, he told himself, it would only

40

take a matter of minutes, an hour at the most, and they, too, would be picking up their heels and doing a bunk. Sadly he concluded Germany was finished. Why try any longer? Just give the *Amis* the damned bridge and that would end the war even sooner.

But that wasn't to be.

Scheller, conscious that his own life was at stake if he failed, turned to the engineer, his own order finished, and snapped, '*Na. Herr Friesenheim – wann?*'

Now it was out in the open, Friesenheim thought; that 'when?' told him all he needed to know. He flashed a glance at his watch. 'Give me an hour.'

Now Scheller looked at his watch. 'That would make it thirteen twenty hours. Agreed?'

'Agreed.'

Immediately Scheller turned to the soldier clerk. 'Write that down. Ludendorff Railway Bridge to be destroyed at precisely thirteen twenty hours. Major Scheller, 67 Infantry Corps. Engineer Captain Friesenheim, Ludendorff Railway Bridge Defence Force.' He gave the engineer a tight little smile. 'That should do it, Friesenheim, don't you think?'

'Yessir,' Friesenheim snapped, telling himself that Scheller was more concerned with saving his skin than the problem of destroying the vital bridge across the Rhine. He dismissed the thought and concentrated on his job. He clicked to attention and touched his right hand to his battered helmet in salute. 'Then I'll get on with it, sir.'

'Excellent. Good man.' Scheller took out a cigarette from an expensive silver cigarette case. With a flourish of his grey-gloved hand, he lit it and puffed out a stream of smoke gratefully. To Friesenheim, the elegant staff major looked like a man well content with the world. He had done all he could, he was safe – let the rest sort out the problems.

He was out of it all. Major Scheller was in a for a great surprise!

Friesenheim pulled his helmet strap tighter. His orderly said, as they stepped out of the shelter of the railway tunnel, 'Think there's iron in the air, sir?' He indicated the heights beyond where the *Amis* would soon appear.

Grimly Friesenheim nodded, pushing his way a little angrily through the stream of refugees. 'We'll soon know, when they start mortaring the entrance to the bridge, or they send in their *Jabos*' – he meant fighter-bombers – 'to shoot up.'

The orderly gave a lopsided grin and crossed himself, saying, 'For what we're about to receive may the Good Lord make us truly grateful.'

'You can say that again, Franz.'

Just outside the entrance to the tunnel, Friesenheim turned the spring key that was supposed to alert the electric system and start the demolition process. Nothing happened. 'Holy strawsack!' he cursed. He gritted his teeth and tried again, his powerful shoulder muscles bulging through the thin material of his shabby grey tunic. Again nothing!

'*Geht es nicht*—' Franz began in the same instant that, hidden somewhere on the other bank of the Rhine, the American artillery thundered into action. Shells and mortar bombs plunged into the water on both sides of the bridge. Friesenheim knew it was interdiction fire. It was the prelude to an all-out American attack. There was no time to be lost.

Sweating heavily now, he turned the key once again. There was no response and now American bullets were ripping the length of the bridge, howling and whining off the steel girders close to where he knelt. For a moment Friesnheim considered whether he should put a team to work repairing the circuit. But almost immediately, he told himself there was no time for that. 'Franz,' he yelled above the roar of the shells and crackling noise made by the rifle bullets, 'do you want to earn yourself a piece of tin?' He meant a medal.

'I've got a drawer full of tin—' Franz began, then he saw the worried look in his old boss's face and added quickly, 'What do you want me to do for Folk, Fatherland and Führer, sir?'

'There's the primacord just over there on the other side of the bridge. You can see the fuse. While I stay in charge here, would you detonate the explosive by igniting the cord by hand?'

Franz shook his head, as if he couldn't believe his own ears. Still he said, 'Yessir . . . if I have to.'

'Then move it before it's too late.'

Franz moved it.

Up on the heights an American machine-gunner must have spotted him. Suddenly a burst of angry white tracer ripped the length of the road in front of the running figure. Desperately the young orderly zig-zagged from side to side, as the slugs tore the wooden planking into matchwood at his flying feet. Friesenheim clenched his fist till his palm hurt. He willed the brave youngster to reach the fuse. Franz staggered. He seemed to hesitate. Then he faltered on. Next moment, sobbing for breath, he was hunched over the primacord. With a hand that trembled wildly, he lit it. It started to fizz and burn. Friesenheim's heart leapt. They were going to do it after all.

Suddenly Franz shrieked. He pitched forward, what looked like a handful of strawberry jam thrown at his face. But the primacord continued to burn. He raised one hand, covered with blood as if attempting to wave at Friesenheim. He never made it. He slumped forward, dead or unconscious, Friesenheim was never able to find out. For in that moment, there came the ear-splitting roar of over six hundred pounds of high explosive going off. Crazily wooden planks were tossed into the air like matchsticks. Girders cracked and buckled. Somewhere a waterline burst and a jet of water erupted from beneath the bridge, which was now swaying wildly and seemed about to fly from its foundations. Friesenheim, his face buffeted by the explosion, gave a sigh of relief. Thanks to the brave young orderly, they had succeeded just in the nick of time. But when the smoke cleared and the swaying had ceased, the engineer officer gasped with shock. The road had been holed in several places and the steel girders twisted into grotesque shapes, but the Ludendorff Bridge was still intact!

Book Two:

The Master Takes a Hand

'I say, chaps . . . Just what are these bloody Americans up to?'
FM Montgomery,
March 9th, 1945

One

'I have one and a quarter million men under my command,' he lectured them. 'My 2nd British Army alone has accumulated 60,000 tons of ammo, and 28,000 tons of other essential supplies. We've got 37,000 British and Canadian engineers involved, plus another 20,000 Yanks. I shall use 5,500 guns of various calibres, which will fire the initial barrage. Beneath that barrage 2,500 pontoons, 650 storm boats, 2,000 assault boats plus 60 river tugs and 70 smaller ones—' Montgomery gulped for breath and his listeners asked themselves, somewhat amused, would he choke altogether before he completed this huge list of figures; for already he was red in the face with the effort. 'All this and much much more,' the sharp-faced beak-nosed 21st Army Group Commander continued, his indignation all too obvious, 'and what do I find? My American allies are trying to cross at various impossible points, almost behind my back, as it were, in shoestring ops launched at the spur of the moment.' Montgomery gave a heartfelt sigh like a sorely tried man. 'All of them carried out so that they –' he meant the US generals obviously – 'can boast, "Today I pissed in the Rhine."' He stopped.

Sitting on their camp chairs in a semicircle around the 'Master', his 'Eyes and Ears', British, American and Canadian, gazed at their boss, wondering if they should

47

snigger or sympathize. For it was clear that Montgomery could simply not comprehend that anyone else might dare to cross the Rhine before he launched his own great, long-planned crossing in two weeks' time. It was simply unthinkable. But in the end the 'Eyes and Ears', as his young liaison officers were called by the 'Master', kept their peace. They reasoned it would be more politic to wait until he addressed them personally.

'Now,' Montgomery continued petutantly, 'I hear some nonsense about General Hodges' 1st Army trying to capture the railway bridge at Remagen. I must say that even if he bloody well does capture it, what good will it do him? It's only a railway bridge in the first place – no good for mass vehicular traffic in the first place, I mean to say.' He gave the circle of young decorated ex-combat officers a hard glance. But none of his veterans, brave as they had been on the battlefield, were bold enough – or foolish enough – to take up the challenge. Besides they knew the 'Master' didn't want answers.

So they sat erect on their hard wooden chairs, listening to the rumble of the permanent barrage in the distance and waited.

'So I'll tell you,' Montgomery continued, 'even if Hodges' men get across, he's going to make bugger-all use of his bridge.' He turned and tapped the map on the easel behind him angrily. 'Look at the road network behind that bridge. Bloody awful! Goes nowhere. All that Hodges can do is capture the autobahn around Frankfurt and what will that get him?' Again an irate Montgomery answered his own question. 'Nothing. It goes in the wrong direction. We're off to Berlin. That's the Supreme Commander's official strategy, isn't it?' For a minute his listeners thought the anger in his high-pitched voice had changed to a note of self-pity.

'The 1st Army, if it gets that bridge and the green light to go ahead, will be heading off in the direction of the bloody Bavarian Alps and what kind of strategic value have they got, I ask you?'

Captain 'Mike' Malone, once a company commander in the US Fourth Infantry Division, turned to his neighbour 'Porky' Posselthwaite, ex-Guards Armoured Division, and whispered, 'The Master's getting a bit hot under the collar today, isn't he, Porky?'

Porky, big, bluff and ruddy-faced like the Yorkshire Squire he had once been, swallowed the chunk of chocolate he had been savouring, and said, 'Rather, Mike. But you can understand the poor chap. After all that planning for the Rhine crossing – and now you bloody Yanks are trying to bounce the river on a shoestring without so much as by-your-leave. Not quite cricket, what.'

The handsome American, his regular features blemished only by the black patch over the socket of the eye which the Germans had shot out in the battle of the Hurtgen Forest the previous November, grinned. 'You and your bloody cricket. Why, it's just good old Yankee get up and go.'

Porky sucked his teeth for the last taste of the milk chocolate he had just swallowed and said, 'At this moment, I bet the Master would agree with that statement – only he'd want the Yankees to go anywhere else but over the Rhine.' Now it was his turn to grin.

For a few minutes more, Montgomery lectured his 'Eyes and Ears' on how he had prepared his own crossing of the Rhine at Wesel down to the very last detail, including contraceptives to put over the muzzles of the infantry's rifles so that the weapons would remain dry during the voyage across; and that he had borrowed heating pads from every field hospital on the Continent. These would be wrapped around the outboard motors of the assault craft to ensure that they would start immediately in the damp spring weather.

As Mike Malone told himself: the Master deserves to be first across; he's planned long enough for every possible contingency. Apparently nothing had been forgotten; everything had been anticipated and prepared for. Save one thing. The Yanks might just steal a march on him. After all, Generals Simpson, Hodges and, above all, Patton in charge of the US 3rd Army, lusted after the kudos of final victory over Nazi Germany. The United States had three men in the field for every Britisher. It was understandable that the American top brass wanted to be seen as the victors and not that 'little fart Monty', as Patton invariably called his limey rival.

'So, gentlemen,' Montgomery was concluding his briefing, 'I want to know what is going on on General Hodges' front. I might have to change my own plans if there is any decisive change down on that stretch of the Rhine. I'll allot each of you to a separate part of the front there. Naturally General Hodges will construe your presence as a kind of spying. But that can't be helped . . . and naturally he wouldn't dare stop you making your enquiries on my behalf. I'd protest to the Supreme Commander, who has given my attack priority, at once.' Montgomery gave them that bold wilful look of his, which Malone knew only too well. It indicated that the Master felt he was a law unto himself; a Jesus who could walk across water if necessary. Finally he said, 'Now then let's see what we can do.' He peered over the top of his spectacles at the paper he now held in his hand. 'Who goes where . . .'

Five minutes later, Malone and Porky knew they had drawn the short straw. They had been assigned not only to Hodges' forward command post, but also to the little Rhenish town of Remagen. As Malone commented to his

British comrade, who was stuffing himself yet again with milk chocolate, 'Porky, if the shit's gonna hit the fan anywhere, it's gonna be at Remagen . . . and if it does, two of us are gonna get well and truly splattered.'

Porky grinned, swallowed the chocolate and made the usual cynical comment he reserved for such occasions, and in these nine months in Europe he'd been in many of them: 'Roll on death, Mike, and let's have a go at the frigging angels.'

Sombrely Mike Malone nodded his agreement. Then Porky took one last bite of the chocolate, slipped their jeep into gear and they were off. They'd soon be heading south for the Rhine and Remagen . . .

As the smoke cleared, the weary infantrymen in Remagen, many of them carrying bottles of wine they had just looted from the little town's cellars, saw that the bridge was still standing. 'Shit,' somebody cried above the chatter of the machine guns, 'the bastards are gonna make us cross after all.'

'You can say that again, buddy,' several voices agreed. 'And that bridge is gonna be one sonuvabitch to cross.' Suddenly a sombre mood fell over the watchers, even those who were already drunk on the unaccustomed wine, which they were drinking straight from the bottle, as if it was beer.

'All right,' the young platoon leader called, waving his carbine, 'let's go, guys.'

The men hesitated. The Germans were pounding the west bank with mortar fire now. Bombs were bursting everywhere. Already most of the half-timbered medieval houses which lined the front were ablaze. Shrapnel hissed and cut the air lethally. Here and there an American went down and urgent cry rose, 'Medic . . . medic . . . over here!'

The company commander, a major, frowned. He rose from his crouching position. 'Come on, you fellas,' he cried above the racket in what he thought was a cheery voice, 'I'll see you on the other side, yeah . . . We'll have a chicken dinner.'

'Stick your chicken dinner up ya ass, Major,' a soldier sneered. Others made even more obscene suggestions about what the major could do with his non-existent chickens.

Now the major was no longer cheery. He saw that no one was about to budge. He snapped angrily. 'All right. No more goddam foolin' about.' He dropped his hand to his pistol holster significantly. 'Move out . . . Get going!'

Reluctantly the men moved to the bridge. Now they could see the holes blown by Friesenheim's explosives. Below, the Rhine foamed and twirled around the bridge's pillars. Someone shouted, 'Let's move fast, guys, and get to the other side. This bridge is gonna fall apart soon.'

With the infantry in the lead, bent double as if they were making difficult headway against a raging storm, the engineers followed, hastily cutting every wire in sight.

But their progress slowed down when twin machine guns opened up from the bridge's two stone towers 100 yards or so to their front. An engineer went down, clawing the air momentarily, as if he were trying to ascend the rungs of an invisible ladder. One of the infantry clutched his knee, bright-red blood spurting through his clenched fingers. 'Fuck it,' he yelped. 'Get me a fucking medic, willya.'

'Sniper fire!' someone called.

'Goddam, why let a coupla frigging Kraut snipers hold up a whole company,' the harassed young lieutenant yelled. 'Let's just get off this frigging bridge. It goes, we all go!'

That did it.

The infantry surged forward, heading straight for the

twin towers. They fired from the hip without aiming. Madly, carried away by the crazy excitement of it, they went down on all sides, bowled off their feet, collapsing in heaps of twitching, writhing limbs. Still the survivors kept on. They knew they couldn't go back now. They couldn't go to ground either. They were fated to continue this lethal dash forward.

They rushed the first tower. A grenade blew the door open. A German soldier crouched on the first flight of steps, machine pistol raised, ready to open fire. He didn't stand a chance. Half a dozen tommy guns opened on him immediately. He was riddled like a sieve, blood jetting from his wounds everywhere. Without a single groan, he tumbled down the steps and lay sprawled out, arms widespread in the brick dust like some latterday Christ on the Cross.

The infantry jumped over his body. They couldn't bring themselves to stand on a corpse even if it was that of a Kraut. They jostled and pushed their way upstairs, ears full of the high-pitched hysterical hiss of a Spandau machine gun hammering away. They slammed open a door. Two Germans knelt there. One was feeding a long belt of ammunition into the MG42, while the other fired, his face glazed with sweat. There were empty cartridge cases piled all around them.

Somebody fired his rifle. The bullet sent up a flurry of stonework just above the machine-gunner's helmeted head. He jumped. His number two hesitated with a new belt of ammunition. Instead he turned, his face suddenly white with shock when he saw the packed unshaven dirty infantrymen. '*Hande hoch!*' one of them shouted.

His hands flew up.

Next to him the gunner cried, '*Los, Mensch . . . Munition—*'

The words died on his lips as he saw his comrade begin to raise his hands. A moment later he did the same. Now the German-speaking GI asked, 'Any more upstairs?'

The gunner shrugged.

He shouldn't have done. The GI slammed the butt of his rifle cruelly between his shoulderblades. The gunner's face struck the Spandau. He started to bleed immediately.

The attackers pushed on. Five minutes later they'd taken the other bridge tower. Ten after that and they had rounded up some 200 German soldiers, most of them elderly, but all tame and ready to surrender without attempting to put up much of a fight.

It was about this time that Ninth Armored's divisional commander, General Leonard, drove up.

Even before he could open the door of his big Packard he was greeted with an excited shout from the regimental commander on the spot: 'We've got the bridge!'

In a joking manner, Leonard snapped back, 'What the hell did you do that for? You know we're not supposed to capture any bridges over the Rhine. Monty and his limeys wouldn't like it. Don't you realize that you've gone and goddamed disobeyed orders.' Then he grinned and said, 'You were absolutely right to do it. Good work. We'll back you up to the hilt, Colonel. Hold on to what you've got and I'll send up every last dough I can lay my hands on till the Top Brass make *their* decision. Suddenly he frowned and said very seriously, 'I wonder if the Krauts have delayed time bombs somewhere hidden on the bridge. Suppose they can blow it up with our guys on the other side . . . We'd lose everything we have over there, you know, Colonel.' He looked very grave.

The other officer remained sanguine. 'We've only got a task force over on the Kraut side, sir. I'm prepared to take the risk.'

Standing listening to the officers' conversation, the Packard's driver told himself: Yeah, he's prepared to take the risk, but he's not the one who might get his head blown off. But he kept the thought to himself. After all generals' drivers usually never got involved in any danger, save perhaps piles from sitting in the driving seat too long. *He'd* survive the war at least.

Leonard sighed. It could be a Kraut trap, he thought, but he, too, felt the risk was worth taking. 'Disobeying orders isn't calculated to get you promotion in this man's army,' he said, almost as if to himself. Then he raised his voice. ''Kay, get to it, Colonel. I'll see what the Top Brass have to say when I signal 'em we've got a bridge.' He took a quick look at the bridge, now shrouded almost completely in the smoke of battle with box-like ambulances carrying the wounded out from the western exit, then he snapped to the driver, 'All right, Perkins. Move it.'

Perkins 'moved it', lickety-split. Like the General he wanted to be out of Remagen fast. As a dedicated coward, as he often described himself to his buddies in the Motor Pool, he knew people were going to get hurt here and he didn't want to be one of them.

Two

The girl was young, pretty and very willing. She was dark, her skin an almost Italianate olive-yellow like so many of these southern German girls close to the border with Italy. She was passionate, too, in a way he had not encountered in the women of his native North Germany, those cool, blue-eyed blondes who felt men had to fight for them and arouse *them.*

Despite her attractions for him, an unhappy Hummel had found that whatever her nature, she had failed to excite him enough to give him an erection. She had tried everything during the night in the pretty little inn on the shores of Lake Constance, which was now the headquarters of the Black Devils. Indeed he felt she might have broken some of the Reich's stringent sexual laws in her efforts to arouse him. Once she had taken it into her mouth and rolled her tongue around slowly and sexually in the fashion of the trained Parisian whores he had slept with in the good years of victory in what now seemed another age. But it hadn't worked and in the end he had patted her gleaming jet-black locks and pulled her head away, saying, 'Thank you, Roswitha . . . But I guess I'm just too old . . . It won't work anymore.'

Hotly she had rounded on him, her lips wet and bright red, crying, 'You are not old, *Kapitänleutnant*! You are a beautiful young man.'

He had laughed at her spirited attack, although that March dawn he had never felt less like laughing. 'Thank you for the "beautiful", *Liebling*. But as for the "young" . . .' he pointed down to his limp penis lolling uselessly on his lean loins, 'that particular beast doesn't look as if he's ever going to bite and bark again.'

Just before dawn as the mist started to sweep across the Lake, as it always did at this time of year, she got up. Completely naked in the dusky-red light from the silken knickers spread across the little bedside lamp, she padded in her bare feet to the mirror. She paused there, looking at herself. She stretched her arms above her so that her little breasts arched upwards, her delightful little bottom pressed back. She stood there, naturally capturing his attention, arms beneath his head silently puffing at his cigarette.

Outside all was silent save for the soft lap-lap of the swell on the shore and the muted rattle of the dixies and cauldrons in the Black Devils' makeshift cookhouse, as the cooks prepared early breakfast for Hummel's young volunteers.

Slowly she bent as if she were about to pull on her stockings. But she didn't do so. Instead she remained thus, her taut young buttocks swelling outwards, the dark crack of her sex and anus clearly revealed. She looked at her shape in the mirror. Very softly she breathed, still looking at the glass, as if she were talking to herself, 'Anything . . . anything you want, *Kapitänleutnant* . . .' She lowered her gaze as if she were abruptly very ashamed, yet determined to undertake what she was boldly offering him. '*Anything?*'

He was touched, not excited. In another age, he would have been beyond himself with lust and desire at the offer. She was offering to do something for him which, if she could rouse his flagging libido by the offer, would inevitably hurt her. He was sure of that. Still it didn't work. His loins remained without feeling. There was no lust in him, just sorrow. 'Come here,' he ordered.

She turned eagerly, her dark pretty face flushed, as if with excitement. She rushed across the narrow bedroom with its squeaky wooden floor and flung her bare arms around his neck. He felt the points of her breasts press against his naked chest. They had no effect. 'Yes?' she demanded in a tight voice.

He laughed, though he had rarely felt less like doing so. 'You're so kind,' he responded and gave her a kiss on her cheek.

'But don't you want—'

He put up his big hand and smothered the rest of her words. 'It's not a question of not wanting.'

'But why?' she asked in bewilderment, forcing his hand away.

He shrugged, his smile vanished. 'I suppose it's the war,' he said, telling himself it was no use attempting to say more.

'It's always the shitting war!' she snorted. 'Why don't you men find pleasure instead of killing each other and ending up like this.' She indicated his naked useless loins.

'Why indeed,' he agreed. He kissed her again.

Outside, the bugler was playing reveille into the address system and the duty NCO was stamping along the cobbled street, rapping at the doors of the Black Devils' billets, crying, '*Aufstehen . . . los – aufstehen*. Hands off yer cocks, on with yer socks!' Hummel grinned at the reference and she gave him a look of both anger and bewilderment. But he didn't try to explain. Instead he said: 'Little bunny, I shall now transform myself from a hopeless lover into the brave Kapitänleutnant zur See Hummel, known behind his back by his disrespectful

58

troops as "Bumble Bee" or even worse names. Give me my underpants, please.'

'And me?'

He touched her cheek with a slightly sad smile. 'You'll come and visit me again . . . I hope.'

'Of course,' she said fervently and attempted to kiss him. He fended her off with, 'Now, let's leave it there. It's too early in the day for emotion, Roswitha.' Even as he said the words, he knew that for him it was already too late.

Outside, his young recruits, all fit, eager young men, were hurrying to the cookhouse for their breakfast of weak ersatz coffee and what they called 'fart soup', a half a litre of thick pea soup, containing (if they were lucky) a slice of 'old man', canned meat reputably made from the corpses of old men from Berlin's many workhouses.

His spirits rose when he saw their keen young faces and how they walked with a swagger, wearing their singlets only despite the chill mist over the lake. For all of his recruits were proud of the insignia on their white vests just below the swastika: the 'pilot' riding on the torpedo, with the legend 'Black Devils' printed below it. Time and time again he returned their salutes with a snap and precision he normally couldn't be bothered to exhibit. His teenagers, volunteers to the man, who already knew that, in the final analysis, the Fatherland expected them to die for it, were a pleasure to the eye. Germany no longer turned out such man in this miserable fag-end of a war that was patently already lost.

His lean face, hollowed out by battle and deprivation to a kind of death's head grew sombre once more. It had taken him six months to replace the losses he had suffered in the attack at Leningrad. By the end of that winter of 1944 he had lost all his replacement crews in their bold suicidal attempts to wreck the bridges leading to Arnhem and to stop the Tommies from opening up the Scheldt entrance to the newly captured Allied supply port of Antwerp. Now he was in the process of doing it again. These youngsters, so full of the confident boldness of youth, embued with the spirit of self-sacrifice, were also fated to die violently soon, if Obersturmbannführer Skorzeny needed them for one of his covert operations. But to what purpose? He frowned hard. In three devils' name – *for what damned purpose*? But as he strode down to the little harbour to inspect the craft, he could find no answer to that particular question.

'*Stillgestanden!*' the same little *Obermaat*, who had sailed with him on the skimmer attack at Leningrad the previous year, barked.

As one, twenty pairs of heels clicked to attention, while the crows in the skeletal trees lining the waterfront rose in hoarse protest at the noise. Rigidly the 'Black Devil' recruits stared into space at some object known only to them.

The *Obermaat* swung round, saluted and bellowed as if he were still back at the parade ground at Muerwik, 'First Training Detachment all present and correct, *sir*!' His wrinkled old face slid into what he supposed was a grin. Hummel knew why. The 'old hare' knew as well as he did, these boys were in no way prepared for what might well soon be expected of them. They were still wet 'behind the spoons', as he might have put it. In the old days, the training of 'pilots' had taken at least six months in the warm waters of the south. Now Skorzeny expected his 'greenbeaks' to be ready for action within the month, although the weather was highly unpredictable on Lake Constance at this time of the year. He dismissed the thought.

'*Danke, Herr Obermaat*,' he cried. 'Stand the men at ease!'

The *Obermaat* gave the command and the young men relaxed a little, shuffling their feet, coughing and in one case breaking wind loudly, as was to be expected on such occasions. There was always one joker in the company who thought it highly amusing to fart on parade in the presence of an officer. Hummel grinned, in no way offended. Let his greenbeaks have their fun, while they still could.

Below, on the water's edge, the two mechanics were now busy removing the tarpaulins from the 'Molch', a successor to the 'Neger'.

While Hummel waited for them to finish, he saw Roswitha come sailing down the hill on her cycle. Despite the freshness of the morning, she was dressed in a wide-skirted floral dress which had billowed up around her delightful thighs to reveal her knickers. Next to Hummel, the wizened *Obermaat* sighed and said, 'Sir, she'd be worth a sin or two.'

Hummel's greenbeaks must have thought so, too. They eyed her young lithe body as she flew by the little parade, waving gaily as she did so, with the lust all too obvious in their faces.

Now Hummel concentrated on the task in hand, as the tarpaulin was pulled back to reveal the 'Molch' or 'Salamander'. It was the right name for an ugly if deadly craft. 'The "nigger" as it used to be called,' he announced, as his greenbeaks craned their necks to get a better view of the secret weapon resting in the water. 'The name was picked by the head of the Navy's secret weapons department, but Obersturmbannführer Skorzeny, who is our commander, decided that "Salamander" is a better designation for her. She is after all a very ugly-looking object.'

There was a little burst of laughter, but the greenbeaks were more impressed by the name Skorzeny: the head of the SS secret commando organization, the 'Hunting

61

Bands'. After all, hadn't the giant scar-faced Austrian SS man kidnapped Mussolini in '43, tried to kill Tito, the Jugoslavian partisan leader the year before, and had attempted to kill the *Ami* general, Eisenhower, two months later? Everyone knew about Skorzeny.

'As you can see,' Hummel continued, 'when you are piloting the Salamander you'll sit under a cosy Plexiglas cupola. You'll feel snug as a bug in a rug . . . riding above two torpedoes . . .' He paused and let them have the full impact of his words: *'Two live torpedoes!'*

They were suitably impressed and the old *Obermaat* snapped swiftly, 'All right, you piss pansies, none o' that chatter in the ranks. Or yer'll be heading for the brig in zero comma nothing seconds.'

Hummel waited a moment and then continued: 'The pilot points his Salamander straight for the target – there's no need for complicated plotting or working out ranges. Then he goes hell-for-leather for it. Naturally he can hardly be seen by the target – he's just above the waves. When he gets within suitable firing distance, he unleashes the tin fishes and swerves as fast as he can to avoid being caught in the explosion and then gets himself out of the way at top speed. Or else.'

'Otherwise he'll get a nasty kick up the arse,' the *Obermaat* chimed in, a cynical grin on his wrinkled face.

'Exactly,' Hummel agreed. 'Now. Last year at Anzio we launched twenty Salamanders at the Allied invasion fleet out in the bay, just south of Rome. Out of the twenty pilots involved, fourteen came back.' Hastily he reassured them with an added, 'Perhaps there were survivors from the missing six – we don't know. But what we do know is this. For the loss of six men we badly damaged an Allied cruiser, sank a destroyer and crippled or sent to the bottom of the sea six thousand tons of

Allied shipping. I think that justified the op, don't you, comrades?'

There was a murmur of agreement from the greenbeaks and Hummel could see they were impressed, poor innocents, who didn't yet know the cruel realities of total war.

'Naturally,' he continued, 'the Tommies and the *Amis* know about the Salamanders by now. They have found the canopies from them in the Channel during our D-Day attacks and probably after our attack on Antwerp. That doesn't matter. Our scientists had been refining and adapting the boats all the time. And we've learned to play tricks. For instance, we have floated empty cupolas at enemy targets and when they had turned to fend off our supposed attack, we have come in from the opposite direction with the real thing. That has surprised them, I can tell you, comrades.'

Like the schoolboys they really were, the greenbeaks chuckled with delight at the trick. It was as if they were back in their classrooms surprising some stuffy schoolteacher with a bucket of water balanced over his classroom door or a drawing pin placed in the middle of his chair.

Hummel let them enjoy what they thought were akin to schoolboy pranks; the reality was vastly different. 'Before we begin today's programme,' he went on, '– and I have a feeling that we won't be training very much longer now the Allies have reached the Rhine,' he noted them casting significant looks and ones of pleasure between each other, but ignored them: he didn't like to feel that he was leading these brave boys, overgrown boy scouts the lot, to their deaths, '– I'd like to show you our newest project, which might come as a bit of a surprise to the enemy, who knows about the older models we have been using so far.' He turned to the old petty officer. '*Obermaat!*'

'*Jawohl, Herr Ka-Lo!*'

63

The little man knew exactly what to do. He picked up the radio loudhailer at his feet and directed it across the lake where through the now disappearing morning haze, they could see the rusty outline of one of the nineteenth-century pleasure steamers which in better days had plied their trade between the German and Swiss sides of Lake Constance. 'Ready at target,' he cried, his voice echoing and re-echoing across the still surface of the lake.

'Ready,' a faint voice answered. 'Abandoning target now.'

'Good. Attack One, do you read me?'

'Attack One, we read you,' an even fainter voice from beyond the steamer came back.

'Count down now!'

From out on the lake came the strangely distorted unreal voice, counting off the seconds to the start of the attack on the steamer now being abandoned by its skeletal crew. Hummel waited, glancing at his watch, wanting to impress his greenbeaks, hoping everything would go off according to plan. For he knew these experimental jobs went wrong often. That was something he didn't want. It might make his young recruits lose the confidence in the Black Devils that he had built up assiduously over the weeks of training.

But Hummel was not fated to see whether the demonstration went well or not. For in that same moment as the muted voice counted: *'Ten . . . ready to attack*, sir', the company office clerk came pedalling furiously along the lake promenade crying urgently, 'Kapitänleutnant . . . express, sir . . . A signal from Obersturmbannführer Skorzeny. Wants to talk to you immediately . . . Führer order, sir . . . *Führer order, sir . . .*' He dropped his machine with a clatter.

Hummel's heart sank. He knew what that meant. Their training was over. They were going into action. The balloon had already gone up.

Three

The previous evening, Skorzeny, the huge SS commando leader with his scarred face that looked like the work of a butcher's apprentice who had run amok with a cleaver, had reached the Führer's HQ too late. The 'Leader' had just turned in and had ordered he should not be disturbed; he had had a stressful day.

But Skorzeny himself had not been able to sleep. Instead he had wandered about the forest headquarters wondering why the Führer had summoned him at this time of crisis. It was thus that he'd bumped into no less a person than the 'Führer's Fireman', whom he had last seen during the Battle of the Bulge nearly four months before. He was shocked by the transformation of the little Field Marshal's appearance. He looked worn and grey and deep lines had been etched in his somewhat gross face. All the same, although it was now two in the morning and Model had obviously had a long journey behind him, he was as active and as pushy as ever.

'Well, you've heard the latest, Skorzeny,' he snapped, as soon as the giant had reported in the usual German fashion, though Skorzeny, as an Austrian, added a little bow to his impressive '*Heil Hitler*' as he towered above the small Field Marshal.

'*Nein, Herr Generalfeldmarschall,*' he replied, realizing

that the latest might have something to do with his being called to the Führer HQ.

'The damned *Amis* have captured the bridge at Remagen,' Model retorted. 'The Führer is besides himself with rage. He wants the heads of the officers responsible on a silver platter by dawn. Now he wants me to attack.' He shook his head. 'Not possible. I'm waiting for Monty to begin his crossing of the Rhine.' He looked up at the giant, his gaze fierce behind the monocle he affected, though he knew the Führer didn't like his generals to wear monocles – '*Monokelfritzen*' as Hitler called them contemptuously. 'It'll be up to you, I imagine.'

'*Me?*' Skorzeny was caught off guard.

'Yes, to use some of those underwater secret weapons of yours, I expect, Skorzeny.'

'Y-yes . . . yes, Field Marshal,' Skorzeny stuttered.

'Nothing, it seems, has agitated the Führer so much since the devilish attempt on his life last year than this Remagen business. I can't counter-attack. I need my 15th Army in position. But you can. I suggest you wake Colonel-General Jodl. Jodl knows what the Führer wants you to do with your chaps . . .'

'And, that's the reason for my call,' Skorzeny now told Hummel over the phone. 'According to Jodl, the Führer's Chief of Staff, he wants me – *you* – to tackle this Remagen business as soon as you can collect your brave fellows and come down here.'

'You can imagine the difficulties and the mean temperature of the Rhine at this time of the year, even in a frogman's suit, after several hours of immersion,' Hummel objected immediately, his head spinning at the thought of his taking his half-trained Black Devils into battle already.

'I know, I know,' Skorzeny said unhappily. 'I told Jodl

all that and made it clear that your frogmen would only take the risk if they thought it a feasible plan.'

Hummel didn't believe the Austrian giant one bit. Skorzeny, he knew of old, was out for glory. If necessary he'd sacrifice his own mother, if he still had one, to advance his career. He tried another tack. 'But I'm sure the *Amis* will be extending their bridgehead along the western and eastern banks of the Rhine by now. After what happened with my people at Arnhem and Antwerp, they'll surely be on the lookout for my Black Devils, don't you think, Obersturmbannführer?' Hummel hated to crawl in this manner. He would dearly have loved to burst out with 'don't bullshit me, Skorzeny.' But he knew he couldn't with Skorzeny being the Führer's blue-eyed boy and enjoying more power than many a full general. But still if he could save the lives of his boys at Lake Constance, he'd crawl like a snake on his damned belly.

'I don't know about that, Hummel,' Skorzeny answered, his voice revealing nothing. 'So far, I gather from Jodl and Model they haven't got enough troops across to extend very far and Model's 15th Army is to begin withdrawing across the Rhine in the Bonn area at six hundred hours this morning, so the *Amis* will have to keep troops in reserve to prepare for a threat from that quarter. Besides what about the "Salamanders"?'

'Salamanders, Obersturm?' Hummel pretended not to understand.

'Well, their pilots don't need to be in the water and they don't need to go to the bridge itself either. They could range in, fire their tin fish at a distance and make a break for it before the *Amis* knew they were even there. Indeed even as I speak to you, I think—'

'But—'

'No buts now, Hummel. Time is of the essence. I'm

seeing the Führer in a few minutes, then I shall ask to be allowed to go to the Remagen front immediately and have a look at the situation personally. Don't worry, Hummel,' he added with that fake Viennese charm of his, sounding to Hummel, the North German, more like a shitting Austrian head waiter than a commander of fighting men, 'I shall be there the whole time when your men attack. I shall personally oversee the whole operation. There will be no risks taken that are not necessary. All right, Hummel, you have orders. Have your men and equipment on the road west within twenty-four hours. *Ende.*'

The phone went dead in Hummel's hand. Skorzeny had made up his mind. For a moment or two Hummel just stood there in the heavily furnished smelly living room which was now his HQ, staring out at the lake, and in the distance his boys engaged in yet another training exercise – obviously enjoying it like the overgrown schoolkids that they really were. He frowned and slowly put the phone down. What in three devils' name was he going to do? How could he save them? For the thought was beginning to unfold in the confusion of his mind that he no longer counted. He was already the past; they were the future. Germany would have need of confident healthy young boys in the dark months, perhaps years, to come after the country was defeated and occupied.

He licked suddenly very dry lips, listening to the joyful cries of his boys as one of them fell from a Salamander into the Lake. Naturally he could refuse to lead the mission against the Remagen Bridge. But what good would that do? They'd probably shoot him, and Skorzeny or someone like him would take over his Black Devils and send them to their deaths. No, that was not the way. His frown deepened. How could he do it?

The soft knock on the *Stube*'s door startled him. It

was Roswitha. She held a package and today she was wearing tight black ski pants that outlined her splendid body perfectly with men's cycle clips at the bottoms.

'Good morning,' she said sweetly, and proferred the package, saying very formally, 'For you, *Herr Kapitanleutnant.*' She gave him a quick curtsey.

He was forced to laugh despite his mood. 'And good morning to you, too Fraulein Hupert.'

Now it was Roswitha's turn to laugh. She handed him the package. '*Blutwurst*,' – blood sausage – 'My grandmother made it during the night. I fixed you a couple of sandwiches. No ersatz in those.'

'Tut-tut,' he exclaimed in mock wonder. 'Black-market killing of the pig at night. That's a serious offence. You and your grannie could go to prison for that.'

'It was our local gendarme, Alois, who slit the pig's throat and ran off the creature's blood to make the sausage,' she said quickly. She saw the quick note he had just begun to scribble after the Skorzeny telephone call. 'Anything?'

'Military secret,' he said, his grin vanished. 'But I'll tell you this, Roswitha, we're leaving.'

'No,' she said. Her bottom lip quivered suddenly and, for a moment, he thought she was going to cry, 'You can't!'

Gently he took her hand. 'Roswitha, you know as well as I do – you've got two brothers in the field – I have no say in what happens to me. I have to obey orders like your brothers do at the front. There is no—'

'But you could find an excuse. We've always got stubble-hoppers coming in to the R.T.O. office where I work, offering excuses – good ones, backed up with documents why they shouldn't be sent back to their units at the front. The wife's sick . . . no one to look after the kids . . . things like that . . .' She stopped, her voice trailing away to nothing, as she saw by the look on his face that it was no use; she was wasting her words.

For a long moment there was silence between the two of them. It was almost as if they had nothing more to say to each other. Then she said, her voice low, as if she hadn't the strength to raise it any higher, 'I shall come to you during my midday break. The men will be eating, too, then.' Without waiting for him to answer, she walked out, her shoulders bent and her beautifully shaped buttocks strangely without their usual sex appeal. It seemed like someone had opened a tap and drained all the youthful vitality and energy from her beautiful body . . .

General Hodges, commander of the US 1st Army, knew he was going out on a limb. Without waiting for approval from his boss, the Supreme Commander, or acknowledging the fact that what he was going to do now would throw a spanner into the works, as far as Monty's great set-piece crossing of the Rhine was concerned, he ordered everything available up to Remagen. Then he commanded that ten infantry divisions should ready themselves to broaden the bridgehead on the eastern side of the Rhine once the area had been stabilized. Finally he bit the bullet and telephoned his Army Group Commander, General Bradley.

'Brad,' he said a little breathlessly once they had been 'scrambled', 'we've gotten a bridge.'

'A *bridge*?' For a moment the bespectacled lantern-jawed Army Group Commander was puzzled, then he got it: 'You mean you've got a bridge intact over the Rhine?'

'Yes, Leonard of the Ninth Armored nabbed one at Remagen before they blew it up.'

'Hot dog!' Bradley exclaimed. 'This will bust him wide open. Are you getting the stuff across?'

Hodges thought it wiser not to tell his boss how many

divisions he intended to send across the Rhine just yet. So he answered, 'I'm going to give it everything I've got.'

'That's fine.'

'I'm having the engineers throw a couple of spare pontoon bridges across.' He added he was sending up two infantry divisions and asked if he should do the same with a third. He didn't mention that he had readied ten divisions in all. He'd do this step by step. After all, there was still Eisenhower to contend with and he had given the priority to Montgomery's crossing in the north. One word from 'Ike' and the whole Remagen business could rebound upon him badly.

'Shove everything you can across,' Bradley urged, 'and button up the bridgehead tight . . . It'll probably take a couple of days to pull enough stuff together for the Krauts to hit you.'

Afterwards, Bradley's staff weren't so sanguine about the new attack. His chief of staff told the Army Group Commander plainly, 'You're not going anywhere down there at Remagen. Besides it doesn't fit into the overall plan.'

'Plan, hell,' Bradley snapped angrily. He was no friend of Monty; this new development might well give him a chance to cock a snook at the 'Victor of Alamein' as he always called the British field marshal contemptuously. 'A bridge is a bridge and mighty damn good anywhere across the Rhine.'

His chief of staff wasn't convinced: 'I was only saying that Remagen wasn't the ideal position to cross that we've been looking for, General.'

Bradley was no longer listening to objections. 'We're crossing,' he snorted. 'We've gotten over the Rhine. Now we've got a bridgehead, for God's sake, let's use it.' And that was that.

*   *   *

71

Mike Malone and 'Porky' knew Bradley's decision by that same afternoon. They, as the 'Master's Eyes and Ears', had always cultivated good contacts among the lower echelons of the Army Group Commander's HQ at Namur in Belgium. Hastily Mike coded a signal to Montgomery's Headquarters and then the two of them decided to hit the road – it was more out of the desire to keep clear of HQ when, as Mike put it, 'the shit hit the fan' than diligence in carrying out their assignment. 'We'll go and find out what's going on at Remagen. With a bit of luck, the Jerries will blast the bridge to kingdom come and then 'the problem will be solved to the Master's satisfaction', as Porky put it, chewing a Hershey bar of which he had picked up a dozen at the Army Group HQ PX.

The journey from Belgium through the Rhineland to the area of Remagen was a nightmare for the two young officers in their jeep. The badly potholed roads, fringed with shot-up German and American tanks and blasted trees, were packed almost solid with trucks and tanks going to the new front. Everywhere there were infantry, weighed down with equipment like pack animals, plodding down the sides of the roads, being hooted at by convoy leaders to get out of the way, with ambulances bearing the wounded from the front, their windows labelled 'PRIORITY ONE – CARRYING CASUALTIES' often shattered by bullets, trying to force their way through the jam heading for the dressing stations to the rear.

But somehow they managed to get through, taking side roads through damaged medieval villages – where the houses were festooned with the white flags of surrender, the civilians hidden behind locked doors and closed shutters, and forcing their way through convoys, 'bullshitting', as Mike Malone put it, military police patrols who tried to stop them with their passes signed by Montgomery personally. That impressed even the hard-boiled tough American MPs.

They arrived at Remagen for the first of the German air raids, which would continue for days thereafter. As the sirens sounded over the battered little Rhenish township, the two of them shaded their eyes against the weak March sunshine and stared at the black dots on the horizon to the east. They came on with slow purposefulness. Battle-experienced as Mike and Porky were, they were struck by their silent sinister approach. Porky even stopped chewing his chocolate.

Below along the river bank and on the approaches to the bridge, the US anti-aircraft gunners prepared to take up the challenge. They swung their 'meat choppers' – their four-barrelled cannon – towards the east and tensed as the mass formations came on and on.

'Stukas,' Porky commented. 'Old-fashioned as hell. But plenty of them.'

Mike nodded, but said nothing.

Now the first flight of the gull-winged obsolete dive-bombers poised over the bridge, seemingly oblivious to the first shells hurrying up to meet them. The German planes seemed to hover there in mid-air. Porky and Mike tensed. They knew what was soon to come.

Suddenly, startlingly, the wing leader appeared to fall out of the sky. He came hurtling down, sirens shrieking, heading in his death-defying dive straight for the ground and self-destruction.

'Holy shit!' Mike breathed in awe. 'What a brave bastard!'

Down and down the Stuka came, flak exploding in brown lethal puffballs all around the plane, tracer criss-crossing the sky to its front. Then when it seemed the Stuka must inevitably go straight into the Rhine, the pilot levelled out.

For an instant the two observers caught a glimpse of him. In his leather helmet and goggles he looked like some alien creature from another planet. But there was nothing other-worldly about the host of deadly black eggs that tumbled from the Stuka's blue-painted belly. The bombs came down in a steady stream and next moment the wing leader was shooting out of range, as the rest of his squadron came hurtling down.

Now the US flak gunners went to work with a will. The Stuka pilots worked without bomb sights and instruments. They simply aimed their plane at the target and released their bombs when they were satisfied that they wouldn't be blown up by their own bombs exploding. That meant they couldn't take evasive action. There was no room for weaving and winding. It was something the gunners took advantage of. The Stukas' course was easy to predict. Thus the slaughter commenced.

Now the gunners started to knock the Stukas out of the sky everywhere.

Abruptly the pale-blue March sky was full of spurts of angry cherry-red flame as planes exploded in mid-air. A pilot, his chute not opening, flew across the river and, near the two observers, burst into a gory mess of broken gleaming white bones like polished ivory set in a red paste. Other Stukas, trailing oily black smoke behind them, their damaged engines groaning and stuttering, tried to escape to the east. But there was no escape. They were unable to gain sufficient height. One after another they smashed into the high naked cliffs on the eastern bank, shattering in bursts of flame and smoke, the metal wreckage slithering down the rock in showers of sparks and dust.

Slowly the sirens began to sound the 'all clear' over Remagen, and the exhausted but triumphant US gunners slumped over their weapons, drinking their looted wine straight from the bottle, smoking hectically one cigarette after another to soothe their agitated nerves and waiting for the next raid to commence. Sitting back in their jeep, Porky put another piece of the too sweet Hershey bar into his mouth and said, 'What now, brown cow?'

Mike Malone shrugged. 'They'll come again. They might even use their new jets. But with the kind of inexperienced pilots the *Luftwaffe* has to use these days, they haven't much chance of knocking out that bridge down there.' He sighed and added, 'The Master isn't going to like it.' Even as he said the words, Malone felt a sense of disquiet. It didn't seem right somehow that he, an American, should be hoping that the Krauts knocked out the bridge which his fellow countrymen had fought and died for. Still, he told himself, there were plenty of limeys who had fought and died in this war long before the USA had entered it; they deserved some of the fruits of victory.

Porky swallowed the rest of his chocolate. 'Mike, if you can work the oracle, we'll stay here and see what transpires, don't you think?'

'Yeah, agreed. I'll see the town major and see if he can fix us up with some quarters. Who knows –' he flashed one last look at the smoke-shrouded bridge – 'the goddam thing might fall down of its own accord . . . though I frigging well doubt it.'

Half a mile away, the SS Commando leader, Skorzeny, frowned and lowered his binoculars. He doubted, too, if the Remagen bridge would be dealt with by bombing or collapsing.

He stroked his nose, deep in thought. At sixteen hundred hours they were sending in a flight of the new Me 262 jet fighter-bombers armed with high explosive and incendiary bombs. The idea was that the jets, which were so fast the enemy anti-aircraft gunners wouldn't be able to keep up with them, would speed in, drop their incendiaries to set fire to the wooden planking placed over the rails of the railway bridge. Then the blaze would be fanned into a raging inferno by the blast of the high explosive. In this way, the *Luftwaffe* commanders hoped they'd start a blaze that would do two things: force the US engineers carrying out repairs off the bridge and give a smoke screen for a German commando raid on the eastern exit. If the *Wehrmacht* could block that, it was thought that von Zangen would be able to counter-attack, once his 15th Army was in position and wipe out the cut-off *Ami* bridgehead on the eastern bank altogether.

Skorzeny didn't think they'd do it. Indeed he didn't want them to destroy the bridge. Even now when the war was almost lost, he wanted to curry favour by destroying that bridge with his own forces. The honour of perhaps the last success for the 'One Thousand Year Empire', as Hitler called his Nazi Empire, had to be his, Skorzeny's.

Convinced he could achieve that aim, Skorzeny went back to his command car. Hastily his signallers started encoding and sending out the urgent messages to his 'Hunting Bands', the tough bunch of paratroopers and SS men who had been the backbone of all his daring operations since the rescue of Mussolini back in 1943, and, in particular, to Lt. Commander Hummel's 'Black Devils'. For the giant Austrian reasoned that if anyone could destroy that bridge down there now, it would be Hummel's young volunteers. Naturally the *Amis*, warned by his operations in Belgium and Holland of the previous year, would expect some waterborne attack on the bridge. He realized that. But if he, Skorzeny, could cover Hummel's assault with a totally different op . . . Slowly like a deadly serpent beginning to uncurl itself, revealing its lethal fangs, ready to strike with lightning speed, the plan started to unfold in Skorzeny's mind . . .

Four

'Let me tell you a tale, Roswitha,' he said softly.
Outside it was already getting dark. The men had packed and they had eaten. He had told the *Obermaat* to issue a ration of 100 grams of schnaps and one bottle of beer per man. That would suffice for a little celebration before they set off west with their Salamanders on the troop train that would leave the little Lake Constance township under the cover of the blackout. 'Firewater and suds for that lot of greenbeaks, sir,' the *Obermaat* had exclaimed. 'Though they're too good for that bunch o' piss-pansies. Besides they can't hold their liquor.'

'Let them have it,' Hummel had appeased the wizened little petty officer. 'Who knows, it might be the first – *and last* – time that they ever get zig-zag.'

'Suppose yer right, sir,' the *Obermaat* had agreed. 'But what a waste on them greenbeaks. Too good for 'em.' And he had gone away shaking his greying head, leaving Hummel to grin.

She had cried when he had told her the news. He had given her a drink of his own ration of the fiery *Korn* and before he had been able to stop her, she had swallowed a huge glass of the clear gin. It had stopped her tears, but now she was maudlin, insisting that she should sit on his knee, clinging to him desperately like some shipwrecked sailor hanging on to a piece of flotsam, as if his very life depended upon it.

'I don't want to hear any tales,' she said thickly, clasping his neck in a choking grip and pecking his cheek with wet kisses all the while. 'I want you.'

Gently he pushed her head away and looked at her brimming eyes and silly beautiful kid's face, telling himself how much pleasure she would have given him once in what was now another age. But that was all past now. In comparison with her, he felt like a doddery grandpa. 'You can't have me. That's why I want to tell you the tale,' he said gently.

'What can a tale tell me about you?' she cried, trying to free her hands, which he had grabbed. 'It's now that's important . . . not then, when . . . Oh, I don't know.' She looked as if she might begin crying again, but caught herself in time, adding in a more reasonable voice suddenly, 'You ought to know better than me. You're an officer and an old hare with all those medals you've won. The war's lost—'

'*Hush*,' he said anxiously, for people were being shot these days for expressing defeatist thoughts like that, 'you mustn't let anyone hear you say such things. It's dangerous.'

'But it's true and what does it matter? All that matter's is now – and love,' she added plaintively. She looked up at him, despair in her young eyes. 'Let me give you some love at least before you go . . . it's all I can . . . do, you know.'

'I know . . . I know,' he said, releasing his grip on her, feeling a little desperate himself now.

Outside in their billets he could hear his young sailors, probably drunk by now, thundering away in one of those marching songs to which the *Wehrmacht* had once marched so boldly, conquering half of Europe in the process. It reminded him again of his duty to them. Now he had a smaller duty to this distraught girl, whom he had attempted to seduce in a half-hearted way – or was it the other way around? He had to wind up the affair, satisfy her that she wasn't at fault; it was him. Now he had to clear the decks with her, just as he would have to with his youngsters when he received the order he dreaded from Obersturmbannführer Skorzeny.

'Nearly two years ago now,' he said in a low neutral voice, 'my wife was killed in the great enemy terror raids on Hamburg. She was three months pregnant at the time. I didn't know it.'

She looked up at him confused. 'But . . .' she attempted but got no further.

'That's it,' he continued in the same toneless voice. 'The beginning and the end of Kapitänleutnant Hummel's personal problem. That day when they took me to Ilse – my wife's body – I got off the world.'

Again she tried to ask a question, but what she asked he didn't hear. For he was back on the terrible July day being led through the burning rubble of Hamburg's Dammtor towards the bank of the city's lake, the Innenalster, where they were laying out the bodies of the dead in their hundreds and their thousands; while in the water those who had been hit by phosphorus pellets from the incendiaries and whose flesh began to burn fiercely once they left the water bobbed up and down, trying not to drown, crying piteously for help.

Not that anyone listened. People had given up listening to other people's pleas for assistance and aid. The horror was too great in that city which burned everywhere with the shattered housing blocks shuddering like theatre backdrops in a sudden wind and the dead lying in the

80

gutters, men, women, little children, like bundles of soaked abandoned rags.

But the fat elderly cop who guided him to where she lay with the others was kind enough under the circumstances. She lay on her side, her upper body draped in a blood-soaked towel. The rest of her was naked. That beautiful body which had given him so much pleasure in the heat of his youth was without a mark, though he could easily see that she was pregnant from the bulge above the dark 'V' of pubic hair.

Suddenly the fat cop had grabbed him by the arm and said in his thick Hamburg waterfront accent, 'Hold both ears stiff, Herr Kapitänleutnant.' He had tightened his grip on Hummel as he nodded to the other cop who was supervising this section of dead being identified.

The other cop swallowed hard. Hummel distinctly heard the sound although all around him was noise – the roar of the flames, the slither of collapsing buildings, the boom-boom of the flak guns in the distance following the last of the enemy bombers as they headed out for the safety of the North Sea.

Hummel tried to free himself from the cop's grip, but the latter was stronger than he looked. Later Hummel thanked God that he was; otherwise he would have fainted clean away at what was now revealed to him. For the other policeman had pulled away the blood-soaked towel to reveal she was without a head. Where it should have been there was a bloody stump with what looked like white stalks of spaghetti protruding from it. He choked and felt the hot bile flood his throat. Just in time he prevented himself from vomiting.

But there was worse to come.

After a moment, while the fat cop clung on to him for all he was worth, so that Hummel's arm hurt under the pressure of his fingers digging into it cruelly, the former asked in a low voice, 'Do you want to see more, Herr Kapitanleutnant, or is that enough?'

'What?'

'The rest of your lady.'

'Yes,' he had heard himself say, hardly recognizing his own voice.

A moment later the other cop had produced one of those fancy hatboxes that had contained the products of the expensive ladies' shops that had lined Hamburg's Jungfernstieg. He paused and then by what, Hummel realized later, was an effort of sheer willpower, opened it. Foolishly Hummel looked at the contents. For many a month later he wished he hadn't. Indeed one minute after he saw what it contained, he wished he had died on the spot, died in ignorance.

It was his wife's head. The face looked in perfect health, indeed more so than normally. Her usually pale face was flushed a healthy red and the lips were an even darker red and full and glowing, as if someone had just applied lipstick to them. But where the torso should have been there was that same gory red stump.

Now he turned and was sick, his shoulder heaving violently as his lean body was racked, so that the fat cop had to exert the last of his strength not to lose him, as he muttered like a fond mother soothing a sick child, 'There . . . there . . . it's all right, Kapitänleutnant . . . all right . . .'

'But it wasn't,' he blurted, staring at her wildly, almost accusingly, 'and it would never be all right again—' His voice broke with a sob.

Abruptly their roles were reversed. It was Roswitha who now attempted to placate him, saying, 'Listen there is a way out . . . something you can do before it's too late.'

He raised his head. 'I can't leave my youngsters!'

'You don't have to,' she assured him.

'How do you mean?'

Over in their billets, the youngsters were bawling a dirty ditty to the tune of a Strauss waltz, '*Steck hinein . . . nicht so tief . . . so ist gut . . .*' While the little *Obermaat* was crying, as drunk as they were now, 'Up the cups, lads. It's gonna be a cold night . . . *Ex* . . . no heel taps.'

'*Ex* . . . no heel taps!' they thundered back, full of the energy and enthusiasm of youth. There was a moment's silence as they drained their glasses and then a great shout, followed by the noise of glass splintering as they threw their 'cups' at the nearest wall.

'Look,' she said, pointing out of the unblacked-out window at the ribbon of twinkling lights on the far shore of Lake Constance. 'Switzerland . . . a neutral country . . . You could be across there – you *and* your boys – and in safety by daybreak tomorrow. If the Border Police tried to intercept you, they'd soon back off when they saw your boats and the weapons they carry.'

He didn't respond.

Urgently she said, 'Hundreds have done it before you. They're the smart ones. The ship's sinking, they don't want to go down with it. Why should you? You've done enough . . . and that –' she hesitated, bowing her pretty head for a second – 'with your wife . . . well that was the last straw. You have every right to take them – *and me* – and go over to the Swiss. The Swiss are not a nice people. All they are concerned with is this.' She made the German gesture of counting notes with her thumb and forefinger. 'But they won't dare send you back to the Gestapo *now*. They're frightened enough about how they've dealt with us Germans and made plenty of money from us throughout the war. Now we've lost it . . .' She shrugged and left the rest of her sentence unsaid.

He knew what she meant. For a second or two he was seized by a feeling of hope, a sense that there might well still be a future for him – for all of them. His boys and the girl. As corrupt sexually as she had become through the war, Roswitha loved him in her fashion. She could change. Perhaps they could even marry, even have children, lead a normal life after years of abnormality—

Then he remembered the cop pulling his wife's head out of the scorched hatbox and he knew there was no future, at least for him. He'd never escape that dreadful day in Hamburg. 'Roswitha,' he said very quietly, in control of himself again. 'I can't do it.'

'But your youngsters—'

'Not even for them. I can't desert the Fatherland now. Remember the old German proverb? *Mitgegangen, mitgefangen, mithangen.** Well I've done all those things. Even if I did think I had a chance in a future beaten Germany, I don't feel I could escape my responsibility for what happened and why we were beaten.' He looked at her, his lean face a mixture of resignation and regret. 'I'm afraid I'll have to hang with the rest.'

'Then you're a fool,' she snapped in a sudden temper.

'Agreed. Then I'm a fool.' Outside, the singing was dying away to be replaced by the soft whistle of the wind across the moonlit lake. It was beginning to grow cold. There'd probably be a frost by morning, he told himself, sensing that a sudden frost had already descended upon his relationship with Roswitha. He could feel it as she edged herself away from his body. The loving, caring look had vanished from her face, too. It was all over between them. A little later, just after he had pulled the black-out shutters and cut off the view of the lake, she went. She didn't kiss

* Literally: 'Went with, caught with, hanged with.'

him, wish him good luck. Instead she said simply, 'Fool,' and with that she was gone, pedalling fast into the cold darkness, as if she couldn't get away from him quickly enough . . .

Five

Mike and Porky sat on the battered overstuffed chairs in the little house on the outskirts of Remagen, eating warmed-up C rations straight out of the cans. 'It's not exactly the Ritz,' Porky, who enjoyed his food in whatever form it came, even out of a khaki-coloured can, declared, 'but it goes down well with a nice bottle of hock.' He indicated the pile of looted green bottles of Rhine wine he had assembled from the cellar.

'Tell that to the doughs,' Mike answered, sticking to the Scotch he was sipping from his hip flask. 'If the MPs don't stop those GIs looting and drinking that wine as if it was neat beer, the Ninth Armored's gonna lose half its strength down with the squits. That hock of yours certainly does go through a guy's stomach like a dose of salts.'

Now it was Porky's turn to laugh. 'Much too good for them, you see. They're not used to the finer things of life.'

Mike gave him the finger. 'Snob.'

'Can't oblige with the finger, old chap,' Porky said, finishing off his lima beans and hash with a flourish of his spoon, licking the instrument carefully before placing it in the top pocket of his battledress blouse. 'Got a double-decker bus up there already, you know.'

Mike shook his head in mock wonder. 'You're a real card, Porky, you know. I always thought before I got to know you limeys that people like you only existed in those ritzy stage plays they used to put on on Broadway before the war. You know, anyone for tennis, chaps, sort of thing.'

Porky took the comment in his stride. *'Noblesse oblige* and all that rot, you know. We have an obligation to keep up appearances even in such primitive circumstances, with not a lackey in sight to bring me a cigar or pour my plonk.' He took another great slug of the hock straight from the bottle.

Outside, the battle for the bridge had quietened down a little. The bridgehead on the other side of the great river was indeed *too* quiet. Both Porky and Mike felt uneasy about that. They had become even more uneasy when they had learned from the Ninth's chief signals officer that his interception teams had discovered that the Germans in that area had gone on radio silence some two hours before. That was always suspicious. As Porky said, 'Always an indication that they're about to go on the attack. Old Jerry's a cunning old bugger, but he still has to learn that radio silence is a dead giveaway.'

Mike had nodded his agreement and said, 'Well, if they do and they recapture the bridge, the Master will be pleased at least.'

Porky didn't comment on the remark. He knew the one-eyed American's divided loyalties on the matter of the Remagen Bridge. Over the last few months since they had commenced serving as Monty's 'Eyes and Ears', they had become firm friends. He didn't want to destroy that friendship because of a matter over which neither of them had any control. Instead he said, 'What about taking a post-prandial stroll, old chap?' He belched politely as if to indicate that he was replete and had enjoyed the meal; now it would be advisable to take a little exercise.

'Post-prandial!' the American snorted in mock exasperation. 'Where in Sam Hill's name do you get such expressions, Porky? Now, don't answer that question. Yeah, it might be a good idea to have a little look-see. Remember the password for tonight?'

'Yes – "Mickey" . . . to which the very original answer is "Mouse".'

The American grinned, then buckling on his .45 and picking up his helmet liner as Army Regulations prescribed, he said, 'All right, Tiger, let us venture forth.'

'Yes, into the twilight we shall go.'

Although the night was dark enough and the river bank was blacked out, there was light enough in the bridge area, where the US engineers were still hammering away, repairing the Ludendorff Railway Bridge and preping the site for an auxiliary Bailey bridge just in case. Searchlights swept the water on both sides at regular intervals and there were patrols, probably made of military policemen, sweeping the promenade on the western side, checking presumably for saboteurs.

Carefully, making sure that they could be seen every time they sensed they were close to a patrol – the military policemen seemed to be particularly edgy this night and the two friends guessed they might well be trigger-happy – they made their way down the river bank and past the bridge.

Neither of them were sensitive men – they had seen too much combat and too much sudden death to be sensitive – yet both felt the eeriness of this place. A couple of hundred yards from where world history was being made, a place of noise and hectic activity, there was a brooding silence; and it was a silence that was more nerve-racking than an actual battle. 'Creepy,' Porky said softly, as they walked along the soft damp turf.

His companion nodded but said nothing. In a sudden

brilliant blue flash of an acetylene torch being used by a welder on the bridge, he had just caught a glimpse of two dead German machine-gunners in their pit. They had obviously been there for days – the Graves Registration blacks were naturally collecting American dead first. Now, for an instant, he thought they were some kind of waxwork dummies, put there to scare people into alertness. But they were real dead men all right; he could see that by the gory mess of the taller man's face. Now it was alive with maggots, as if the flesh was moving. His stomach fell like an express elevator. He turned away swiftly, as Porky repeated his conclusion – 'bloody creepy, isn't it?'

'You can say that again, buddy,' the American answered grimly. 'That's for fucking sure.'

Some seventy-five yards away, Pfc. Joe Bagnio pulled off his rubber, wiped his penis pleasurably with his sleeve, tied up his flies and said, '*Schokolade* or *Zigaretten*? . . . *Zehn.*' He held up the fingers of both hands to make quite sure that the woman with whom he had just had intercourse was quite clear that that was all he was paying her for her services – ten smokes. After all, all it had been was a quick 'knee-trembler'. A real fuck in bed would have been worth a pack at least.

The girl from the village pulled up her knickers and tied her garter more firmly around her left woollen stocking, which had begun to slip during the rough handling he had just given her. God, she told herself, the *Ami* had more arms than an octopus. 'Ten . . . I understand,' she said in halting English. 'One for Papa, eh?'

'Yeah,' Bagnio agreed. 'One for your old man. You did a good jig-jig.' He slapped her plump peasant bottom in appreciation and gave her another 'Lucky'.

He began to proposition her for the morning, when he'd come off guard. Perhaps she had a real bed where he could give her the old one-two and then get some real shut-eye, away from the other guys. '*Doschlafen mit me?*' he began . . . '*Beaucoup schokolade* . . . Plenty jig-jig.' He worked his clenched fist back and forth obscenely to make his intention. '*Du kiss Soldats—*' He stopped short. Something was moving in the darkness to his front. Instantly he was alert, 'jig-jig' forgotten at once.

'*Was ist los?*' the peasant girl asked, though she knew exactly what the matter was.

He ignored her. Old soldier that he was, he could sense the impending danger. He picked up his M1 rifle hastily and then, bending low, swung his head from left to right.

It was an old trick. It was the way to spot something on a dark night: a darker object against a lighter darkness. And there it was. Something moving on the surface of the water close to the bank.

'*Was ist los?*' the girl repeated her question.

'Shit is los,' he hissed. 'Come on . . . back over here. There's somebody on the water and I don't think it's frigging Father Christmas come to give me frigging Christmas presents.' Hastily he pulled her deeper into the shadows, the girl muttering, '*Nix mehr* jig-jig . . . Go home *zur Mutter.*'

'Ferk yer mother as well,' he hissed, flicking off the M1's safety catch. For suddenly he realized he was in serious trouble. There were other bastards out there and he didn't need a crystal ball to know they were Krauts.

He knelt. He knew this way he would present a smaller target. He took a deep breath and challenged: 'Who goes there?'

'*Scheisse!*' an angry voice retorted.

The sentry wasted no more time. He pressed the trigger. Scarlet flame stabbed the darkness. Someone shrieked.

There was a splash like someone falling backwards into the Rhine. Next moment there was the stutter of a German Schmeisser. Slugs cut the air all around the crouching man. Next to him the girl yelled hysterically. She went down screaming, her plump left breast mangled in a bloody pulp and lay moaning on the towpath.

'Shit on the shingle!' the sentry cursed. If he got out of this and the top sergeant found him with the woman and reasoned – rightly – that he'd been fucking her while on duty, he'd be for the high jump. They'd probably send him back to Fort Leavenworth prison for the rest of his natural-born days. 'Beat it,' he urged her. 'For Chrissake, girl, beat it while you've got a frigging chance!'

But neither the wounded girl nor Pfc. Joe Bagnio had a chance this night. The stakes were too high. Just as he bent down to try to help the girl to her feet so that she could stagger off into the darkness and safety, the cruel blade struck him in the back. He gave a great gasp. A searing pain shot through his skinny Italian body like a red-hot poker being thrust into an open wound. Next moment he was on the ground and someone was straddling him, pressing the muzzle of a pistol to his neck just behind his right ear.

A second later his world exploded into nothing and the girl clutching her shattered breast trying to run for it before it was too late was mown off her feet by a cruel burst from a Schmeisser at close range which virtually sliced her in two . . .

Trained combat soldiers that they were, Porky and Mike dropped to one knee, weapons appearing as if by magic in their hands. They knew that last sound all too well. 'Kraut grease-gun,' the one-eyed American hissed, heart thudding excitedly, as he clicked off the safety catch of his Colt.

'Schmeisser,' Porky, .38 already in his fat fist, agreed.

'To the front . . . two o'clock . . . Can you see? . . . Somebody moving over there.'

'Got ya!' Malone breathed tensely. He felt the adrenaline surging through his body, powering it with that old electric energy that a man needed in combat. 'You take the path?'

'Yes.'

'I'll go the bank. Come in from the right flank. Watch yer step, old buddy . . . and keep your eyes peeled.'

'Like the proverbial tinned tomato,' Porky whispered, imperturbable as ever.

They parted, preparing to come in on the flanks of whoever was out there in the heavy darkness. All had fallen silent once more and Porky could hear his own breathing, as he heaved his bulk forward slowly and carefully. It sounded to him like a small elephant approaching. Yet once again, he told himself that he had to lose weight, but those Hershey bars—' He stopped short.

To his front a shadow had detached itself from the deeper shadow cast by the embankment. He tightened his grip on his revolver and stared hard. He was trying to make out whether the shadowy figure was wearing the typical US helmet. Americans wore helmets all the time, even if they were working in an office in some headquarters miles behind the fighting front. If the figure didn't wear one, it was likely that he was a Jerry. Then the question was should he challenge or shoot the bugger straight-off without warning. In this type of confrontation, he knew from his past experience in the line, there was no time for hesitation. The one who fired first usually won the fight.

The figure was without a helmet!

Porky's hand holding the revolver was abruptly wet with sweat. Should he fire? Should he challenge?

The decision was made for him. Over in the river there

was the sudden splash of paddles and a soft voice queried, '*Eckhart . . . los dalli-dalli . . .*'

Porky hesitated no longer. He pressed the trigger. The .38 jerked in his hand. There was the sudden stink of burnt cordite. Next moment, the shadowy figure yelped with pain and staggered. In the same instant that Porky fired and the figure broke from cover, he could hear the unmistakable sound of Mike's heavy Colt, followed an instant later by the high-pitched burr of a German Schmeisser.

Abruptly everything was violent action and chaos. From the river the paddles splashed in and out. A man ran down the embankment. Mike's Colt spat fire. The running man threw up his arms with a wild shriek, as if appealing to some god on high for mercy. But this night God was looking the other way. The man splashed into the shallows, groaned once and lay still, head in the water.

Porky ducked as the Schmeisser burst split the darkness just over his head. Later he swore he'd felt the heat of the 9mm slugs as they hissed by him. 'Cheeky bugger!' he cried in indignation. Next moment he fired himself and the Schmeisser fell silent. Mike came sliding down the embankment firing as he slithered to a stop. 'The Kraut bastards are everywhere,' he gasped. Next moment he ducked as a burst came from the river, missing him by inches.

'Get your bloody big Yank nut down!' Porky cried and pushed him to the ground, firing with his other hand. 'Standing there like a spare prick at a wedding.'

Despite the danger, the American grinned. Old Porky was a real pal – that explained his anger. Down on his knees, he commenced firing too. But the intruders, whoever they were, had had enough. Firing bursts at regular intervals, making the two officers keep their heads down, they vanished into the middle of the great river. There they

93

ceased firing and as Porky and Mike rose to their feet to peer through the gloom, it was clear they had almost reached the other side. Then the sound of the paddling died altogether and they knew, whoever the Krauts and whatever their task had been on the US side of the Rhine, they had completed it . . .

'A Kraut patrol,' the MP officer said, flashing his torch beam around the scene of the little skirmish, while his white-helmeted MPs spread out a little fearfully, or so it seemed to the two officers, with their carbines and tommy guns held at the ready. It was as if they half-expected to bump into the rest of the German Army at any moment. 'We've had three already in this sector in the last two days. Or –' he flicked the white beam in the direction of the man Porky had shot – 'it could be Krauts trapped on this side trying to get back to their own lines . . . there are hundreds of the mean S.O.B.s still on this bank.'

'Yeah,' Malone said sarcastically, 'and Captain, if you keep flashing that torch around like that, one of them out there might just take a potshot at you.'

'Jesus H.,' the MP captain swore and clicked off his flashlight immediately, leaving them blinking in the sudden darkness. Thus it was that an hour later they made their startling discovery.

The MPs had loaded the the bodies they had found on to what the Germans called a '*Bollerwagen*', a wooden cart used for towing objects by German farmers, and transported them to the nearest cottage, where someone had found a petroleum lantern and lit it so that they could all gather round in the tight kitchen and gawp at the bodies as if they were viewing some strange creatures from another planet.

Porky could understand the big beefy military police-men's wonder, for under their tunics, the two dead men

94

wore skin-tight rubber suits complete with great awkward-looking flippers that might have appeared amusing if they had not been worn by two very dead Germans. He could hear them muttering among themselves about the strange gear and especially the flippers, whispering, 'Never seen anything like that before . . . kinda like the big fish you see in the ocean . . .'

But Porky's wonder had turned to alarm once he had seen the rubber suit and the military patch the dead men wore on the shoulders of their tunics. He nodded to Mike, who got the signal immediately and followed the tubby Englishman outside, leaving the MPs to continue staring at these strange dead Germans.

'Do you know who they are?'

'The Krauts, Porky?'

'Yes.'

Malone shook his head and adjusted his patch hastily as it slipped and revealed the empty socket which he hated.

'Skorzeny's boys,' Porky whispered, once Malone had closed the cottage door behind him.

'You mean the Mussolini guy?'

'Yes, a real thug, Mike. We've already had one report of his naval unit operating on the 9th Army front before the Jerries managed to blow the two bridges which were still intact up there.'

'And now Skorzeny's boys are after this one here at Remagen, Porky?'

'Yes, it looks like it. This patrol – that's what I think the Germans were – was checking the terrain. They have to have a site to launch their weapons – torpedoes, mines, high explosives floated down in containers and the like, and the site can't be too far from the bridge because the Rhine in this section winds and wanders all over the place.'

'You mean they want a straight run up to the bridge so that they can deliver the weapons?'

Porky nodded sombrely. 'Yes, that's the buggers' plan.'

But the bluff Yorkshire squire was wrong for once. Obersturmbannführer Otto Skorzeny had something totally different in mind for Hummel and his youngsters of the 'Black Devils' Squadron . . .

Book Three:

The Glory Boys

'If anyone can stop the Americans, it's you, Skorzeny,
and your brave boys.'
Adolf Hitler to Otto Skorzeny,
March 12, 1945

One

'There is always hope as long as one believes, my dear Skorzeny,' the Führer said, placing his shaking hand on the giant's arm. 'And I still hope. For if I did not, and you know this better than most as a fellow Austrian, then Europe must surrender to the yoke of the eternal Jew.' He started to tremble once more.

Hastily Skorzeny said, '*Mein Führer*, please do not agitate yourself so much.'

'But I must, my dear Skorzeny. For I fear what will happen if Germany – Europe – succumbs to Jewish-American capitalism. In a few years he will have exterminated our intelligentsia and by robbing the mass of our ordinary citizens of their natural leaders, the Jews will make them ripe for the slave's lot of permanent subjugation.' He licked his parched cracked bloodless lips.

'*Jawohl, mein Führer, aber*—' Skorzeny attempted to interrupt the sudden flow of words and try to get down to the reason he had been summoned to Hitler's headquarters yet again. In vain. Hitler, as always, persisted in the making of one of his rambling speeches.

'We shall not allow the Jews to get away with it,' he continued with abrupt fervour for a man who was so obviously sick. 'As a young man, a boy really, I first became aware of this great Jewish plot when I arrived at your native city, Skorzeny – Vienna. There I first met the eternal Jew. That changed me from being a weak-kneed idealistic provincial to a fervent dedicated anti-Semite. There I learned that there wasn't one single form of filth or profligacy especially in Vienna's cultural life without at least one damned Jew being involved in it. Then if you cut into such an abcess, however cautiously, you found a maggot in the rotting body – and the maggot was always a Jew.'

The Führer continued to rant and although Skorzeny agreed with him, he barely understood half of Hitler's supposed philosophizing. Yet he knew instinctively that the Führer was right. The war was not merely being fought for a German victory – no, it was being fought to stop eternal Jewry destroying European culture, even the world's.

'As often in history,' the Führer was saying, 'Germany is the great pivot in the mighty struggle. If our people and our state become the victim of these bloodthirsty and avaricious Jewish tyrants of nations, the whole eath will sink into the tentacles of this octopus . . . if Germany frees herself from this deadly embrace, this greatest of dangers to nations will be wrested from the whole world . . .' His voice was breaking and he was running out of breath, but still Hitler persisted to the end with his diatribe against the Jews. 'We must fight on till the bitter end and ensure that the Jews are massacred,' he gasped, 'for I believe, in doing this, I am acting in accordance with the will of the Almighty Creator.' He raised his forefinger, as if he were addressing the mass audience at the Nuremberg Party rally back in the good days before the war, and ended with, 'By defending myself against the eternal Jew, Skorzeny, I am fighting for the work of the Lord.' Suddenly, startlingly, the energy and fire vanished, as if someone had opened some invisible tap in his frail sick body and he seemed to shrink to become yet again the old ill man, doomed to an imminent death that he was.

Skorzeny was not a sentimental man. But now his dark eyes filled with abrupt tears and his heart went out to the leader who was obviously dying on his feet. He said, '*Mein Führer*, rest assured that *I* and my Hunting Bands will not let you down in your struggle against the dark powers of evil. We will turn the Americans back at Remagen . . . we shall destroy that bridge of theirs on the Rhine, even if it takes the life of every last one of us.'

Weakly, Hitler, his face pallid and drawn again, said, 'Well spoken, my dear Skorzeny, well spoken. I know you of all people will not let me down as so many of my supposed loyal followers have done in these last terrible months.' Now his voice was without conviction. But Skorzeny did not notice. For he was himself now carried away with emotion.

'*Mein Führer*,' he boomed, 'we – I and my staff of the Hunting Bands, have worked out a plan which we believe confidently will ensure the bridge at Remagen – the last over the Rhine this day – will be destroyed before the Americans can make full use of it.'

'Remember, Skorzeny, speed is of the essence, every hour we delay will see more and more of the enemy crossing Father Rhine.' He used the old German expression for the great river, perhaps to emphasize the place the Rhine had always had in German hearts, ever since there had been a united Reich.

Skorzeny allowed himself a careful smile at the phrase, then he was businesslike again. 'We have planned the unexpected, *mein Führer*,' he continued, 'in the same military tradition that you yourself created back in '39.'

'Excellent, excellent. As I have always maintained,

never let your sword grow cold. Strike while it is still hot. And the scheme?'

'This, sir. The *Amis* expect us to continue to retreat from the Rhineland and go on the defensive on the eastern bank of the Rhine. That is their usual sort of conventional thinking.'

'Yes, yes,' Hitler urged, somewhat impatient now.

'We, however, intend to go on the offensive to ensure that when we launch our waterborne attack on the bridge at Remagen, we have a base on the correct side of the Rhine to commence – and the correct side happens to be *in American hands*!'

'Very good thinking, Skorzeny,' Hitler agreed, 'but a major crossing of the Rhine from east to west is impossible under present circumstances. We don't have the firepower to cover such an undertaking and I doubt if the Navy could provide the boats in time. All roads to the bridge and the rail links too are under constant attack by those damned American air gangsters and their terror fliers.'

Skorzeny looked very pleased with himself as he announced somewhat pompously, 'But it wouldn't be a waterborne attack, *mein Führer*. I intend to use my chaps from the SS Fallschirmjäger Battalion. They are totally committed to the plan of attack, cost what it may. You may say, sir, they are eager for some desperate glory.'

Hitler's weak, worn face lit up at the phrase. 'Eager for some desperate glory,' he echoed. 'What a splendid phrase. Now, Skorzeny, do tell me more about – er – your Glory Boys, I pray you . . .'

'You know, gentlemen,' Montgomery told his assembled 'Eyes and Ears', 'this must be in the strictest confidence.' He looked at a weary Malone. 'And I expect my American officers to keep mum, too . . . Now as I was saying,

Churchill once said of General Bradley, the US Army Group Commander, "a sour-faced bugger, who won't listen".' He allowed himself a taut little smile, but his eyes didn't light up; the matter, he thought, was too serious for that. 'Well, I don't know about the sour-faced, but once again he's proved to be a bugger who won't listen.'

Porky looked at his friend Mike. Montgomery was usually very frank with his young liaison officers, but rarely this frank about his fellow senior commander. He wondered why.

'The Supreme Commander, General Eisenhower,' Montgomery went on, his thin hawklike face looking distinctly sour, 'has ordered that his bridgehead at Remagen must not exceed a depth of ten miles. Naturally Ike is afraid the bridge there might collapse and leave the soldiers on the other side cut off and wide open for a German counter-attack. From what Malone and "Porky"' – Monty enjoyed making digs at the British Guards officer's bulk – 'report, the Remagen bridge is very near collapse as it is, though Hodges is trying to get two Bailey bridges in place before it does. That, however, does not seem to concern General Bradley. Again he's not listening, not even to the Supreme Commander. Already he's got parts of five US divisions across and I am sure he's not going to allow them to be compressed into that ten-mile limit. They'd be sitting ducks for German artillery.' He paused and stared around the circle of their intent young faces, as if searching there for something, known only to himself.

He let them wait for a while and then said, 'I am not in the picture, naturally. There has been no official contact between General Bradley's HQ and mine. However, Malone and Posslethwaite tell me they've gathered that US 1st Army is now pushing through the hills and woods on the other side of the Rhine, heading for the autobahn at Frankfurt. Naturally, although the 1st is going in the wrong direction, the Jerries won't allow him to get a foothole on the motor highway leading south to Munich. So they'll attempt some sort of counter-attack. Now . . .' He swivelled and tapped the big map on the blackboard behind him and as he turned his young officers grinned cheekily at one another. They knew only too well just how much the Master loved to give strategic lectures on infantry tactics. Obviously they were in for one now. Hastily Porky slipped a large chunk of chocolate out of his pocket and hurriedly put it into his mouth before the Master turned back to face them. A chap needed some nourishment at moments like this, he told himself.

But for once the 'Master', who never allowed himself to be disturbed if he could avoid it, was not able to give one of his school-masterly briefings. For to the relief of the young officers sitting there in the cool March air, the headquarters' Chief Signal Officer no less, a full brigadier, came rumbling across to where Montgomery stood waving a 'flimsy' and crying, 'Sorry to disturb you, sir . . . But it's urgent. Straight from the S.L.U. people . . . Sorry, sir.'

The 'Eyes and Ears' were impressed. It was very rare that they were present when the 'Master' received a communication from the 'Special Liaison Unit' – the S.L.U., the Air Force outfit which was located near 21st Army Group HQ, yet which lived a life of its own, cut off from the Army HQ personnel.

Naturally being the bright young men that they were, they knew there was something very strange about the S.L.U. First it was Royal Air Force, but had no dealings whatsoever with the other RAF units attached to the Monty HQ. Its personnel was stand-offish, armed at all times, and even the common-or-garden signallers were all sergeants or even flight sergeants. The S.L.U. messed alone, took their

104

pleasures, whatever they might have been, alone at night and guarded their camp as if they were concerned that the rest of Monty's forward HQ was some kind of dangerous enemy outfit. As the Army personnel said, 'They're a fishy bunch, bloody fishy.'

Now, a full brigadier was delivering one of their messages and, as was usual, in the background an RAF squadron leader hovered, fully armed and ready to seize the 'flimsy' from the 'Master' himself, once the latter had read it to bear it away in a steel box to – they knew not what particular purpose.

So Montgomery read the message, went through the customary procedure, handing it to the brigadier, signing that he had received it, while the brigadier passed it to the sombre-faced, suspicious squadron leader, his hand on his pistol holster, as if he expected to be attacked at any moment. The latter saluted, did a smart about-turn and hurried off to the S.L.U. area, where rumour had it all these strange messages were immediately shredded under the watchful eye of a similar armed guard.*

Montgomery turned back to his audience, all thoughts of a little lecture forgotten now as he beamed at them with his emaciated foxlike face,

'Gentlemen,' he announced in obviously high good humour, 'it appears that our problem at Remagen seems about to be solved.'

Malone frowned at that 'our problem at Remagen'. But he was too intent on listening to what the 'Master' had to say to dwell on the words.

'I have just received a report from one of our secret

* What the 'Eyes and Ears' were watching of course was the delivery of one of those war-winning Ultra decodes from Bletchley Park, England.

sources that that thug Skorzeny – you've heard of him, of course – has signed an order alerting both his air transport squadron, KG 100 at Hildesheim, and his notorious SS Parachute Battalion at Fraedenthal – the same battalion that tried to capture Marshal Tito in Jugoslavia last year. You realize of course what that means?'

Some of the 'Eyes and Ears' obviously didn't. Montgomery tut-tutted like the old schoolmarm he could be at times and enlightened them: 'It means that the Boche are going to try an airborne attack on the Remagen bridge – and I shouldn't be surprised if they don't succeed. They've had plenty of experience of such attacks starting in Holland back in '40.'

'But sir,' Malone raised his voice.

'Yes, Malone?'

'Won't 1st Army know about this supposed attack and be prepared?'

Montgomery looked at the one-eyed American, as if he were incredibly naive. 'I don't suppose they will. After all it's just an educated guess on my part that this is Skorzeny's intention.' He smiled. 'And even I can be wrong, you know, Malone. But not very often, of course.'

The American was flabbergasted at the 'Master's' cold-blooded approach. What he was really saying was that he wanted the Americans at Remagen to be caught by surprise in the hope that the bridge would be destroyed and all new efforts to cross the Rhine would be concentrated on his set-piece assault in the last week of March. In essence, Montgomery was prepared to allow ordinary American Joes, simple GIs, to he killed in order to achieve his own ends.

Malone was no innocent. He knew the ways of generals, British and American. They were all glory-hunters, out for headlines, fame and promotion. But in his nine months of combat at the front he had never witnessed such a blatant example of this as now. His face reddened with anger. As Montgomery turned to go back to his caravan, he rose again and snapped, 'Sir . . . sir, a question.'

Hurriedly Porky grabbed at the back of his 'Ike' jacket. 'For Pete's sake, Mike,' he hissed, 'sit down and don't make a bloody fool of yourself!'

'But don't you know what the Master's up to? He's gonna sacrifice my fellow Americans—'

The departing Montgomery must have caught some of Malone's hissed outburst, for he paused in his stride and said over his shoulder to Malone standing there, red-faced and with his fists clenched, 'Oh and yes, Malone, you and that chocolate-eating friend of yours from the Guards, get back to Remagen toot-sweet and be ready to report. You know the scene best.' And with that he was gone . . .

Two

N ow the first of the nine Junkers 52s carrying the SS Parachute Battalion turned south-west over the Taunus hills and started to lose height. Behind it the others followed suit, their pilots' eyes glued to the lumbering transport's exhaust flames, the only guide they had for this daring midnight drop.

Below, the German countryside slept, though on the horizon where the new front was, there was the silent pink flickering of the permanent barrage. The war was still there; there was no doubt about that. Not that the lead pilot guiding the squadron had time to concern himself with the fighting front. His whole being was concentrated on getting the squadron on target for the daring jump. Then his mind was full of Skorzeny's last words to him before take-off at Hildesheim. 'Drop my glory boys accurately, *Herr Major*, and there's the German Cross in Gold in it for you . . .' He had looked threateningly at the *Luftwaffe* officer. 'Fail and you'll find yourself leading a punishment battalion in the east. And you know what that means?'

The major did. That meant certain death, clearing some minefield or the like under fire and without mine detectors.

Now as they left the hills behind, he could see the dull silver glint on the horizon. It was the Rhine. They were approaching their objective. He nodded to his co-pilot.

108

He nodded back. He knew what to do. He reached out and pressed the button. Back in the packed fuselage, the red warning light glowed abruptly and the parachutists in their camouflaged coveralls started to pick up their bits and pieces ready for what was soon to come.

The 'Auntie Jus', as the crews called their old transports lovingly, droned on towards their date with destiny. Skorzeny was about to take the battle to the Americans with a force that hitherto had been unbeatable and one which still believed that the Fatherland could win.

Now the Rhine was coming up fast. The lead pilot, the *Luftwaffe* major, knew that by now enemy radar would have picked up his formation and soon he could expect flak. But Skorzeny's team had worked out certain plans for fooling the *Amis* at least till he had dropped the SS paras when, with a bit of luck, he'd head hell-for-leather for the safety of the nearest *Luftwaffe* base of Cologne-Wahn.

He came even lower. He knew that the paras couldn't jump at a height below 150 metres, but he'd get nearly as low as that to try the first element in the attempt to put off enemy defences. 'All right, Jakob,' he snapped to the pilot, 'let them have it – at the double. *Dalli . . . dalli!*'

The young second pilot needed no urging. At this stage of the war, he didn't want to die for Folk, Fatherland, Führer. He wanted to live to be old. Hastily he pulled open the flap window to his right. Ice-cold air flooded the cockpit. He didn't notice, it seemed. Now he started tugging the silver chaff out of the sack at his feet and scattering it into the darkness below. It was a British invention tried out by the RAF at the great raid on Hamburg in '43, but the *Luftwaffe* had adopted it, for the Allies didn't seem to have found a counter-measure against their own invention. Now the cloud of silver chaff should be sending the *Ami* radar operators into a crazy tizzy as suddenly what

109

seemed to be planes would be appearing on their radar screens everywhere.

The major grunted his approval. He pressed his throat mike. 'Once we're over the Rhine,' he said to the co-pilot, 'the gunners will start firing at us without the benefit of radar. But with a bit of nifty footwork, our flares might do the trick until we can get rid of those SS arseholes in the back and be off back home to mother.'

'You can say that again, sir,' the co-pilot agreed and prepared for the second stage of their deception plan prepared for them by Skorzeny and his planners at Friedenthal . . .

Skorzeny fumed. For six hours now, his Friedenthal HQ had lost contact with the Hummel convoy coming up from the Lake, the goods train carrying the Black Devils and their vital torpedoes. 'In three devils' name,' he raged at his staff, 'where the hell are they? The airborne op is already under way and they are lost somewhere in the wilds of Franconia.'

'The airborne operation is going well, *Obersturm*,' one of his officers reassured him. 'Last news was they are crossing the Rhine. It shouldn't be long before KG 100 is dropping the SS Parachute Battalion—'

'*Damned idiot!*' Skorzeny turned on the unfortunate staff officer, sallow scarred face flushed an angry red, 'what good is the airborne op if there is no Salamander outfit to follow it up?' He raised his mighty fists like steam shovels above his head in the Austrian gesture of frustrated rage. 'Where . . . oh where are the damned Salamanders?'

The Salamanders and their young crews were at that moment in the middle of nowhere stalled at some god-forsaken country station, surrounded by hundreds of former Soviet prisoners-of-war who were baying for their blood like the animals they had become.

The long goods train had stopped with an abrupt lurch, tumbling the still half-drunk youngsters out of their bunks, to the sound of wild firing, while the crazed voices of the elderly guards outside cried, 'For God's sake, let us aboard before it's too late . . . The shitting Ivans have eaten the shitting guard dogs, complete with *Haut und Haar!*' – skin and hair! 'If you don't let us on, they'll shitting well eat us as well.' Under other circumstances a suddenly wakened Kapitänleutnant Hummel might have smiled at the panic-stricken guards' plaints. But not this dawn. It was all too obvious that the guards were fleeing for their lives, as if the Devil himself was after them. Which in a way was true. For the ragged Russian POWs, many of them still wearing the fur caps in which they had been captured, were streaming across the fields, striking the slower guards down mercilessly and immediately robbing them of whatever food and tobacco they could find on the dying old men.

Hurriedly the youngsters grabbed their weapons, while the surviving guards scrambled aboard and lay panting on the wet floors of the carriages, like ancient asthmatics in the throes of a final attack. Now the Ivans, who had collected the weapons the guards had thrown away in their panic-stricken flight from the POW camp, were beginning to snipe the stalled troop train.

Crazed and hungry as they were, blind to anything but the desire for the food they knew the train contained, the Russians were still cunning enough to make sure it wouldn't continue. Already they had pulled the civilian driver and fireman from their cab and were in the process of shattering the poor unfortunates' skulls with their own shovels, as they grovelled there in the blood-red light cast by the open door of the firebox.

At the end of the train the leather-masked air lookout in

his raised box had turned his machine gun on the killers, but even as their comrades were hit and tumbled writhing and twisting in their death agonies, other Russians took their place in the murder of the civilians.

Now wide awake and with a pistol clenched in his first, Hummel sensed a feeling of apprehension, yet despair at the human condition. The Russians had become animals. But who had turned them from captive enemy soldiers to these wild primeval creatures beating the two middle-aged unarmed men to a bloody pulp like that? The answer was obvious. His fellow Germans had.

But Hummel knew that there was no time for such moral considerations. The Russian POWs would undoubtedly massacre him and the rest of his youngsters if he didn't do something drastic immediately. Without the driver and fireman, who were now undoubtedly dead, they were trapped. Should they abandon the Salamanders and try to make a run for it? He dismissed that possibility immediately. Even if they killed scores of the Russians, there were still hundreds more of them, prepared to sacrifice their lives for the chance of getting food to cram down their starving throats. No, he decided swiftly, they'd have to stay and defend the train the best they could. Perhaps someone had already raised the alarm and rescue was on its way. But he had an uneasy feeling that wouldn't be the case. As the harsh little voice at the back of his mind rasped cynically: 'If you believe that, Herr Kapitänleutnant Hummel, you'll believe anything.' Then he was aiming his pistol, firing shots to left and right. The battle of the troop train had commenced in real earnest . . .

'Prepare to jump!' the *Luftwaffe* major commanded, shouting above the roar of the Junkers' three engines. Now the lead plane was a mere 150 metres above the ground. Below, it flashed by in a black haze; the drop was going to be dangerous.

'Helmets on!' the sergeant major in charge of the SS paras ordered.

Obediently the tough veterans in their camouflaged overalls, the silver SS runes, which had once brought fear to the whole of Europe, gleaming at their collars, pulled on their helmets.

'Ready to jump!' the major yelled, watching the red light intently, waiting for it to turn to green.

The sergeant major waddled to the open door. He grasped the supports on both sides, legs spread in the jump position. The slipstream clutched at his cheeks. He felt them fluttering like small flags in the icy wind. To his right silent white clouds had suddenly appeared in the darkness. For a moment he couldn't make out where they had come from so abruptly. Then he realized what they were. *Flak!* But the guns were far off-target. The radar-confusing chaff had done its work well.

Below he caught glimpses of the Junkers' shadow as it flashed across something white. A village street. But he had no eyes for the village. His gaze was searching for the level space they had been briefed about further on. That's where they were supposed to drop in a nice tight group. He prayed for a moment that the *Luftwaffe* arseholes would put them down in a professional stick. They'd need every man they could – *on the spot* – once the *Amis* discovered this little Trojan Horse in their midst.

Abruptly the green light flashed on. The major didn't hesitate. They had lost the flak. But one never knew. At all events he was not going to wait around, with the rest of the squadron coming in right behind for the tight drop he had promised the Viennese thug, Skorzeny. 'Go!' he yelled at the top of his voice.

113

The SS sergeant major didn't hesitate. He went through the door as if plucked out of it by an invisible hand, his arms spread out wide. Next moment he had vanished into the noisy darkness.

In rapid succession, the SS paras shuffled forward and threw themselves one after one behind him.

Now the rest of the squadron came in with the sound of a swarm of enormous hornets, rising to a throbbing, vibrating drumming. Hastily they released their cargoes. In an instant the night sky was full of camouflaged canopies drifting into the gloom below with not a single shot being fired at them. The first phase of Skorzeny's plan had been carried out with total success.

Three

'*C*hrist *on a crutch!*' Malone swore, as he saw the wire stretched tightly across the road between the two pines. 'It's them?'

Even before Porky, sitting next to him in the front seat of the jeep, was aware of the wire, the one-eyed American had hit the brakes. With the rubber of the tyres squealing and smoking, he swung the jeep round and went barrelling back up the country road they had just come down, with both men tensed ready for the first shock of steel slugs slamming into their backs.

None came and when they were safely round the bend in the fir forest, Malone slowed to a stop, reaching for the carbine in the bucket next to him as he did so. But he didn't turn off the jeep's overheated engine. Now it ticked away like a metal heart in the brooding silence of the forest, while Malone caught his breath and Porky, his Sten cocked and ready, too, now refrained from answering that overwhelming question for a few moments till Malone was ready and composed once more.

They had been at Hodges' HQ in Spa when the reports of German aircraft had started to flood in six hours before. Then it had still been dark and although the HQ had sent up little light artillery spotter planes they had been unable to report anything relevant. It had been the same with the 30th Anti-Aircraft Brigade in Germany. They stated their

115

radar had been swamped and blinded by a large drop of chaff and they had not been able to report accurately what was going on in the air space west of the Rhine.

In the end the two 'Eyes and Ears' had set off into the night to try to find out for themselves; for that was the kind of information that the 'Master' delighted in. He dearly loved telling his fellow army commanders, especially if they were American, what was going on in their own command. But during the long tiring night journey to the Rhine, Porky had noticed that his old friend didn't say very much. It was as if he were preoccupied with his own thoughts and the bluff ex-Yorkshire squire felt he knew what they were: this attack on the bridge which Montgomery was still withholding from 1st Army's staff.

Once when they had stopped for what Malone called rather primly in the American fashion 'a comfort stop' and they had been standing side-by-side urinating into a roadside ditch, Porky had ventured, 'Don't take it to heart, Mike. The Master'll pass on the information in due course, I'm sure he will. After all, you Yanks are our Allies.'

Malone had not been forthcoming. As he finished, he grumbled, 'It just isn't right. Hell, some American boys are going to get killed by this, if Monty doesn't spill the beans soon.'

Thereafter he had relapsed into a brooding silence, muffled up in his jeep coat, as Porky took the wheel for the rest of the journey. Porky, for his part, decided to drop the subject; it was safer that way.

Now with the new dawn and the nerve-tingling surprise of the wire stretched across the road in the general area where the planes had first been spotted hours before, the two old comrades were their usual selves once more. They had to be. For they knew that old irregular warfare trick indicated to them that in the wood somewhere there

116

were experienced German soldiers: a fact they felt was confirmed by the knowledge that whoever had stretched the wire across the road had not fired on the fleeing jeep and given their position away.

Now Porky broke the heavy silence: 'All right, Mike, do you think it's them? Paras dropped by those transports?'

'Yeah. I'll bet my bottom dollar it is.'

'Yes,' Porky said, 'I agree. Indeed –' he sniffed the damp morning air with his big nose – 'I can smell old Jerry in there somewhere. Yes, very definitely a Jerry smell about it.'

Malone shook his head in mock wonder, no longer angry at his old friend. 'Sometimes,' he commented, 'I don't think you limeys take this war seriously.'

'Perhaps. But as dear old Oscar Wilde said, God rest his pansy soul, "Life is too serious to be taken seriously." All right, Mike.' The Englishman was business-like now, 'What's the drill?'

'A little recon first, Porky. I think we'd better find out if your nose is not deceiving us. Then we report to the authorities.' Suddenly Malone was very serious. 'To my way of thinking, this is going to be the secure base from which the Krauts are going to launch their waterborne attack on the bridge.' He wasted no more words, ''Kay, old buddy, let's get on the stick.' He gave Porky's considerable bulk a significant look, and added. 'This time we hike.'

Porky sighed like a much tried man, 'Oh my sainted aunt. The things I do for jolly old England. All right, Mike, let's – er *hike* . . .'

'General der Infantrie von Hoffmann sat on his saddle chair, his right hand dug deep into the pocket of his voluminous riding breeches, the other holding the phone.

The young whore at the other was speaking very slowly and sexily, as if she were savouring every word she spoke, knowing as he had often told her, 'When you talk dirty like that, my dear, you make an old man very happy.' At this particular moment he was indeed happy.

'I shall be wearing black silk French knickers and frilly lace garters,' she was saying in that provocative naughty manner of hers, breathing in hard between phrases in the most delightful fashion. 'But naturally, Konrad, you mustn't be a naughty boy and try to remove them from my body, however much I'd like you to do so.'

'And if I do so?' he said somewhat breathlessly, his right hand groping ever deeper into his pocket.

'You see, there you are – being naughty again. I'm afraid I have no other alternative but to punish you.'

'You mean like you did when I touched your beautiful little titties?' the old general's breath was coming in rather hectic gasps now.

'No, no,' she said, her voice very firm now. 'That was just a warning. This time it will be off with your breeches, shirt tail up and a damned good whacking.' She ground her teeth like a caged wild beast. 'Do you hear – a damned good whacking!'

'Oh, you are so cruel!' he gasped.

'No, it wouldn't be cruelty, just deserved punishment of the most severe kind, I can assure you. Your rank and position will not save you this time.' Her voice rose threateningly and the general thought he might faint with the excitement and sheer sexual pleasure of the conversation. 'Naughty boys deserve to be punished over and over again for their wickedness until they have learned to improve their behaviour . . . Do you understand me, sir?'

'Yes, yes,' he quavered in the same instant that the door of his office flew open to admit a giant of an SS officer, whose eyes blazed furiously and seemed about to pop out of his head at any moment. The general took his hand out of his pocket in a flash, 'What kind of damned impudence is this –' The words died on his lips, as the giant threw back his greatcoat to reveal a burly chest covered in medals with the highest of them all dangling at his throat, the Knight's Cross of the Iron Cross.

'Obersturmbannführer Skorzeny!' the giant thundered, his voice full of threat.

'G-General der Infantrie v-von Hoffmann,' he managed to stutter, while over the phone the whore's voice was saying, 'You may have your way with me, General . . . for sordid pleasures. But you will pay for it, indeed you shall. Not with my poor woman's hand . . . but *with the whip*!' The old general jumped as if the whore might have just run the lash across his withered buttocks and put the phone down hard. '*Skorzeny!*' he echoed, voice suddenly full of awe. He was about to jump to his feet to welcome the Führer's favourite when he remembered the slight swelling in his breeches. Instead he smiled, revealing his yellowed false teeth and said, 'This is an honour, Obersturm.'

Skorzeny wasn't impressed. 'You are responsible for Military District Five?' he snorted.

'I am.'

'Well, General, if you are, what do you know of my missing troop train? On the Führer's own order, that train with its complement, was supposed to be on the Rhine this very morning. But it has been stopped and is without communication with Military District Five's own railway transport communications HQ. That is your responsibility. How do you explain it, sir?' It wasn't a request; it was an order, and the general knew it. Suddenly he was frightened.

The previous July Hitler had ordered German field

119

marshals and generals to be strung up and strangled to death – *slowly* – for supposed treachery. He was old but not fool enough to believe that Hitler wouldn't do it again if he felt the need to do so. He swallowed hard and reached for the phone, 'I shall make immediate enquiries, Obersturm,' he snapped in the style of the young divisional commander he had once been.

'There is no need,' Skorzeny said icily.

The old general's hand, covered with liver spots, dropped from the phone as if the apparatus had suddenly become red-hot. 'How do you mean?'

'I mean this. While you have been fornicating here in that disgusting manner I was just witness to, neglecting your job, I have already found out what has happened. A large number of those sub-humans, the Russians, have broken out from their POW camp at Crailsheim. They are ravaging the country all about, looting and ravaging, raping our decent German women. Now, it seems, they have held up my troop train and are threatening to overwhelm it by sheer weight of numbers.' Skorzeny shrugged eloquently. 'As you can see, I am alone, I have flown down here with my pilot to find the train. I've have found it. But what can I do? I have no men. You have. Why aren't you mobilizing them? Where are your alarm companies and battalions? They should already be on their way to deal with these impudent Slavs and saving my poor fellows for the task which the Führer himself has given them.' He drew himself up to his full and very imposing height, as if he were speaking to the Leader personally.

Von Hoffmann felt himself go red. How dare this SS thug talk to him like this? he asked himself. Once he had commanded nearly twenty thousand men in battle. In the old war he had shed his blood six times for Imperial Germany. Now this supposed hero, Skorzeny, with his haughty Viennese manner, which in his own youth had cut no ice in Prussian Berlin, was talking to him like a shitting lance corporal in the sanitary corps.

He pushed back his chair. 'Let me show you something, my dear Obersturmbannführer,' he said, his fear suddenly forgotten. He was an old fart with no future anyway; what did it matter if Skorzeny didn't like his manner and had him strung up by some of his fellow SS louts? 'Let me show you my alarm companies – it just happens they are on parade at this very moment.' Without waiting for Skorzeny's approval, he grabbed his cap and his stick and limped to the door. After a moment or two's hesitation, the puzzled head commando followed.

Behind the barracks complex, the one-eyed cripples, the officers with empty sleeves, those with their faces an angry pink and ravaged by disease, were trying to get the black-clad boys into some semblance of order. They were eager enough and proud of the antiquated weapons that they had just received from the quartermaster stores, but they had little idea of real military discipline. They giggled, they talked in the ranks, played with their weapons, as if they were some new-fangled toys, and seemed to ignore or not notice the orders rapped out by the handful of wounded officers who were to command them if they were ever – God forbid – ordered into battle. The old general swept his shaking hand along their ranks and said with a note of angry bitter sarcasm in his reedy voice, 'My alarm battalion!'

Skorzeny gasped audibly. 'B-but,' he stuttered, 'they're a bunch of . . . Hitler Youth. There can't be one of them who is older than sixteen.'

'*Fifteen!*' the old general corrected him. 'Those in the long pants are fifteen.' He turned the knife in the wound, not caring now a tinker's damn what might happen to him. 'But, Obersturm, you may rest assured that every last one of them would not hesitate a single moment to lay down his life for the Führer and – er – our noble cause. They will fight to the last man and the last round. For they still believe.' He gasped from so much talking and felt suddenly ashamed of what he was saying just in order to take the wind and piss out of the Austrian thug. He drew a deep breath and controlled himself. 'Men . . . comrades of Number One Alarm Battalion Franconia. I have the honour to present to you one of your heroes, Obersturmbannführer Otto Skorzeny, who, as you all known has carried out so many brave and bold missions for our German Fatherland.' He stepped back and gave Skorzeny the benefit of his false-toothed smile.

Otto Skorzeny was not the most sensitive of men. Irony was wasted upon him. But he could see the decadent old general was attempting to make fun of him. Yet the senile creature had forgotten one thing: the fanatical sense of self-sacrifice which imbued German Youth after twelve years of being indoctrinated with the National Socialist creed. The kids facing him were exactly that – kids, armed with a ragbag collection of weapons. Yet Skorzeny knew these same kids could still knock out an enemy tank with their one-shot rocket launchers or hold some disputed barricade until their ammunition ran out. In short, whatever the old general thought to the contrary, these boys in their black short pants would die more bravely on the battlefield for Adolf Hitler than many a hardened 'old hare', his chest covered with orders for bravery.

Skorzeny no longer hesitated. 'Young soldiers of Adolf Hitler, I have a mission for you . . . a desperate one, I must confess, one from which some of you will not come back . . . Hence I am not asking you to obey my command to go and do battle . . . No, I am going to ask you to volunteer.' He raised his voice even more, while the crippled officers and General von Hoffmann watched with growing amazement – and alarm. 'All those young comrades prepared to fight in this desperate hour when our Holy Germany's fate is at stake, take one pace – *forward*!'

As one, the whole of the assembly of Hitler Youth kids stepped forward, skinny chests thrust out proudly, chins raised as they had seen their soldier heroes do in the *Deutsche Wochenschau* – German newsreel.

'*Bravo. . . bravo, jungs!*' Skorzeny exclaimed in delight. 'I knew in Germany's hour of need, our beloved Führer could rely on his Hitler Youth.' He wasted no more time. He swung round to face General von Hoffmann, who seemingly couldn't believe the evidence of his own eyes. 'General, ensure that those brave boys are given transport immediately.'

'T-Transport . . . to where, Obersturmbannführer?' the old man stuttered.

To the front naturally, General . . . to the front . . . *Where else?*'

Four

Porky moved surprisingly quickly for such a heavy man. He ducked under the dripping, fog-shrouded firs and threw himself into a ditch. Behind him, Malone, who had been covering him, bent, doubled forward and dropped the next minute into the ditch. Both of them, containing their heavy breathing the best they could, cocked their heads to one side and listened intently.

For a moment or two they could hear nothing save the steady mournful drip-drip of the moisture falling from the rigid lines of firs marching across the Rhenish plain like spike-helmeted Prussian grenadiers. Then they caught it. It was the sound of someone digging in. Malone nudged his old comrade. 'Push on?' he whispered.

'Yes . . . push on.'

Gripping their weapons more tightly in hands that were now damp with perspiration, the two of them advanced carefully, bent double, in the direction from which the sound of spades hitting the earth and tree roots was coming.

Now they could just make out movement from behind the next row of trees. Malone paused, pressed his mouth close to Porky's ear and hissed, 'There seems to be two of 'em . . . setting up perimeter defences.'

'Machine gun,' Porky hissed back. 'Can just make it out.' He stopped and ducked low abruptly, as a tall, helmeted German came out of the trees, opened his flies and urinated in a hot gush of yellow liquid against the nearest tree. He gave a sigh of relief, did up his flies and vanished again to his digging.

Porky waited a while before saying, 'Did you see his collar dogs and helmet, Mike?'

'Yes,' the one-eyed American officer answered grimly. 'SS . . . SS paratrooper to be exact.'

'The best of the bunch at this stage of the war,' Porky agreed. 'All right, what's the drill now? Do we do a bunk and tell the powers-that-be what we've discovered?'

Malone considered for a moment. 'That would be the safest. But it would help the boys back there more if we knew what the Krauts were up to in detail, Porky.' He looked hopefully at the Guards officer.

Porky recognized the look. 'Got you . . . you mean, take a prisoner . . . Like the one who just did a Jimmy Riddle. He was a Scharführer – a sergeant to you. He'd be the sort of bloke who might know something more than the ordinary squaddie. SS non-coms – thugs that they might be – usually are pretty highly trained, ready to take over if their officer stops one.'

'Agreed.'

Minds made up, the two officers began their stalk. Now as they got closer to where the two men were preparing the perimeter machine-gun position, they could hear the muted sounds deeper in the wood that indicated that these SS paras who had landed so surprisingly in the midst of the American 1st Army were preparing a regular defensive position: the scrape of an entrenching tool on tree roots, the slither of soil being shifted, the squeak as rolls of barbed wire were unstrung. As Malone guessed, the SS were attempting to keep their position hidden as long as possible. They wouldn't try offensive action until the attack on the Remagen Bridge commenced. After all, he reasoned that was why they had made this bold drop right in the middle of the US defences.

They were close now. By hand signals, Malone indicated that Porky should crawl to the right of the two Germans preparing their position; he'd take the left, where the SS NCO who had urinated against the fir was busily engaged hacking out the machine-gun pit.

Now he tucked away his pistol. In its place he drew the fighting knife from the back of his webbing belt. It was a fearsome weapon, for it combined a razor-sharp blade (complete with serrated edges so that it would make the biggest possible jagged wound when stuck in someone) and knuckleduster commando grip. Someone punched on the jaw with a set of brass knuckles like that would go out like a light.

Still Malone knew the SS NCO was powerfully built and, like the British commandos, he'd be trained in all the dirty tricks that could be employed in unarmed combat. What counted was catching the SS thug off guard in the very first minute and doing the dirty on him there and then; Malone could count on Porky taking care of the other man. Porky might be slow-moving but he packed a wallop like that of a kangaroo.

He drew ever closer. Hardly daring to breathe, he stalked the unsuspecting SS man while he hacked away with his combined pick and shovel entrenching tool, his powerful shoulder muscles rippling cruelly beneath the thin material of his airborne coverall. Malone told himself, he looked one very tough hombre indeed. There'd have to be no messing with him. He'd have to nobble him the first go round. Or else . . .

The bodies of the dead Ivans littered the fields around the

stalled train; there must have been at least thirty of them in front of the sweating anxious Hummel. But still they came on, a lot of them unarmed, as if they were so greedy for food and loot that they were prepared to tear the train apart with their bare hands. Hummel guessed they had been drinking looted schnapps or something powerful of that nature. That had been the way they had fought out on the Eastern Front, bombed out of their minds with vodka, blind to the lethal dangers of battle.

Under other circumstances, Hummel knew his young-sters, as few as they were, could have held them. But there was one great problem that was increasing in magnitude by the instant. They were running out of ammo. For their kind of warfare, the Black Devils didn't need much ammunition, just enough for their personal weapons. Now they were hammering away, using up their bullets at a tremendous rate. And it was necessary. For if they didn't keep up the volume of fire, the ex-Russians POWs, who seemed to be everywhere, would sneak up and board the train. Hummel didn't need a crystal ball to know that once the Ivans managed to get into the train in any force, his youngsters didn't stand a chance. Then it would be man against man and his Black Devils were hopelessly outnumbered.

Thus he was forcing and dodging his way down the compartments, urging his youngsters to conserve their ammunition, 'Aim and fire only when you know you can't miss,' he kept exhorting them, dodging as yet another burst of fire splintered the thin fabric of the coaches as if it was made of matchwood. But he knew even when he shouted the order over the angry snap-and-crackle of the fire fight that as soon as the Ivans attacked in strength again, shouting that dreaded '*Krasnaya Armya*' of theirs followed by the great bass roar '*URRAH!*', his youngsters would blaze away for all they were worth once again.

Casualties were mounting too. Not that they were particularly serious, mainly flesh wounds and splinters from flying glass and wood, but all the same his defensive fire was weakening and he thanked God again for the leather-masked lookout in the observation tower at the rear of the stalled train who was hammering away with his Spandau and keeping the Russians at bay.

All the same, Hummel knew their luck couldn't hold out for ever. If the Ivans managed to put the machine-gunner out of action – and he was still able to cover the whole train with his protective fire from his elevated position – then the 'clock would be in the pisspot', as the old hares phrased it. What then? The animal-like Russians, brutalized by the terrible years they had spent in the German camps, would show no mercy on their former captors. They'd massacre them out of hand then and there.

It was about then, when Hummel had begun to grow desperate, that their terrible salvation occurred. On the slight rise to the east of where the troop train was stalled, a lone figure appeared. For a moment Hummel's heart missed a beat. Not more Ivans, the frightening thought flashed through his brain. But the sound of that well-remembered tune from his own youth told him that this was not another Russian. How often had he once marched proudly to that same bold song as a youth leader back in the mid-thirties. '*Unsere Fahne flattert uns voran*' . . . 'our flag flutters before us'.

Next to him the old *Obermaat*, dark blood trickling down his wizened face from a wound in his right temple, exclaimed, 'It's the shitting Hitler Youth!'

It *was* the 'shitting Hitler Youth'.

Marching in a column of three like toy soldiers, a stream of boys in the black pants and light shirts of the Hitler Youth came into view now, all of them carrying rifles and other weapons over their shoulders, as the officers shouted commands and the NCOs started to form the column into a skirmish line.

'Holy strawsack!' the *Obermaat* hailed them. 'Rescued by a shitting lot of boy scouts.'

'Not yet,' Hummel cried grimly, as the Russians turned to face the newcomers. 'Not yet I'm afraid . . .'

The Hitler Youth took their time. As their seniors chivvied and bullied them into some sort of order, their fife-and-drums marched forward and lined up behind the tall blond youth carrying the blood-red flag of the Third Reich. As anxious and concerned as he was, Hummel gasped. Next to him the little *Obermaat* said in wonder, 'What in three devils' name are they going to do, sir? . . . Surely,' he answered his own question, 'not parade?'

Hummel was too shocked to reply.

Next instant, he had the answer. Led by a one-armed officer, who swayed badly as if he were drunk when he took up his position at the head of the skirmish line, the fife-and-drum band broke into a parody of the great Prussian march 'Frederich Rex'. The officer gave a hoarse cry and the ragged line moved off down the hill towards the train.

The Russians turned to face this new opponent. Hummel could see from the rapacious delighted look on the escaped POWs' faces that they couldn't wait for the short-panted boys to come into range. The *Obermaat* said it all when he exclaimed, 'Great Crap on the Christmas Tree, sir, the Russkis will eat the poor little piss pansies alive. God, why did their stupid shitting mothers ever let them out?'

But there was no answer to that question, as the band played bravely, the tall boy with the flag waved it proudly from side to side and the boys advanced, their faces set in the look of those dead heroes they emulated – straight to their death.

For what seemed an age Hummel was rooted to the spot. He was so shocked by the sight of the short-panted kids heading for eternity that he couldn't think straight; indeed he could not even think at all. But he knew he had to. He had somehow to prevent the impending tragedy.

Then his brain snapped back into action again. He knew he could order his men to use up the rest of their ammunition on the Russians. But already they were moving back to meet the new challenge, to the line of trees running parallel to the railway line where the troop train was stalled. Soon they'd be at the extreme range of his riflemen and, being sailors, most of them were poor untrained shots as it was; they'd simply waste ammo. What was the alternative? And he knew there had to be one or the poor stupid kids would be massacred.

Then he had it. It came to him with the suddenness of a vision. He knew it would cost him one of his precious torpedoes – and Skorzeny wouldn't like that one bit. 'Skorzeny can go and piss in the wind,' he whispered half aloud.

'What's that, *Ka-Lo*?' the little *Obermaat* took his gaze off the dreadful scene unfolding on the heights to their front.

Hummel ignored his question. Instead he snapped urgently, 'Get a team together. Your strongest chaps. You know that spare torpedo already on the—'

'Why, sir?' the *Obermaat* looked at him, as if he had suddenly gone completely mad.

'Don't ask questions. Just get to it . . . *at the double, now*!'

Five

'**O**kay, punk,' the gross man from the US Counter-Intelligence Corps growled, twisting the unlit stump of his cigar from one end of his slack mouth to the other. 'Let's have some answers from you and make 'em quick.' To emphasize his haste, he hauled back with his pudgy hand and slapped the *SS-Scharführer* across the face – hard.

Malone winced and Porky stopped chewing his piece of chocolate, he was that shocked by the display of naked brutality.

But the tough SS non-com whom they had just brought into Ninth Armored Headquarters for interrogation was not impressed. He looked up at the fat civilian, if that was what he was, and smiled cynically. '*Arschloch*,' he said quite distinctly.

Next to the CIC man, his interpreter said, 'He called you an arsehole, Hermann.'

'The Kraut cocksucker,' the interrogator said slowly, his pig-like pink eyes boring into the prisoner. 'Well, we'll see who's gonna be sucking cock by the time this little question-and-answer session is over. Yessir, we'll see.'

Leonard, the Ninth's commanding general, said hastily, 'Well I'll leave you to it. Please let me know what you find out immediately.' And with that he fled the room. Porky

131

and Malone knew why. He didn't want to be present when the rough stuff commenced.

The CIC man addressed the little Jewish interpreter, who had gone pale himself at the realization that this wasn't going to be the standard interrogation when you might threaten dire punishment if the prisoner didn't answer the interrogator's questions but never carried those threats out. 'Tell the Kraut bastard, I want to know – one, how many of the other Kraut bastards there are in there in the forest. Two –' he ticked the number off with a fat finger like a hairy pork sausage – 'what kind of heavy armament they have and three, when the fun and games are supposed to commence. Got that?'

'Yes, got it, Hermann.' Hastily the interpreter posed his questions and it was clear that he was more afraid of the CIC man than he was of the SS thug he was questioning.

But his questions met with no response, as the two 'Eyes and Ears' half suspected they would. The Hermanns of this world didn't realize just how tough the regular SS troopers were. Both Malone and Porky had seen wounded SS troopers refuse blood transfusions in captivity because they'd rather die than be 'contaminated' by blood that might be Jewish; and it was obvious that the *Scharführer* had recognized the interpreter for what he was – a German Jew – and treated him with contempt accordingly.

'Well?' Hermann queried, chomping on the cheap PX cigar.

'He refuses to talk, Hermann,' the interpreter said a little fearfully, as if he felt the big bully of a CIC might well start on him at any moment.

'Does he now?' Hermann said, very tamely for him. 'Well, well, ain't that fine and dandy.' He smirked and then said, 'What about getting me a pail and a broom, son?'

The interpreter looked mystified. But he didn't ask

132

questions. Instead while the *SS-Scharführer* glared at the fat American civilian and the officers looked on in bewilderment, the CIC man sucked happily on his unlit cigar, as if all was well with the world and his own life was just a bed of roses.

A moment or two later the interpreter returned with a broom and one of those shining white pails that Porky had noticed before in German cottages; the locals used them to fetch water from the well or outside pump and placed them on a bench near the kitchen range to be used when called for. The CIC man thanked the little interpreter with exaggerated courtesy and said, 'Ask him the same question again, willya please.'

The man did so.

All he received as an answer was the same scowl as before. Hermann took it in his stride with, 'So you're gonna hold out on me, eh? Well we'll see about that, buddy.'

With surprising speed for such a fat man, he lashed out, caught the SS man by complete surprise and before the latter realized what was happening to him had tied him securely to the chair with his own belt, which they had taken off the German as soon as he had been brought for interrogation. The *Scharführer* glared up at the fat man, eyes full of burning hate. Not for long. Next moment the CIC agent had slapped the pail over his head and cut off that look.

Hermann looked at the two younger officers and said, 'Now get a load of this, boys. When I used to work for the NYPD, the guys used to say, old Hermann could get even a frigging mummy to talk. And I think the guys were right.' He reached for the broom, snapped the head off in a brisk gesture and then, spitting on the palms of his pudgy hands, swung the pole back, as if he were wielding a baseball bat. 'Strike One!' he cried pleasurably.

Next moment he whacked the pail a tremendous blow. Inside it the prisoner gave a muffled yell as his head slammed to one side.

Hermann grinned happily and hauling the pole back again, struck the pail a second terrific whack.

The two 'Eyes and Ears' were horrified. Porky clenched his fists with anger and said, 'You can't treat a prisoner like that, even though he is SS!'

The CIC man looked at the red-faced, stout Englishman calmly, 'Listen, limey,' he said, 'I'm the boss man here. You keep your big limey nose out of it, d'ya hear?'

Malone tapped the butt of his pistol. 'And you keep a damned civil tongue in your head, if you know what's good for you.' His hand remained on his pistol butt and Hermann realized that the officer with the black patch over his eye meant business.

'Say, Captain,' he whined, 'I'm just doing my duty . . . I'm trying to save the lives of our boys, don't forget.'

'I don't,' Malone replied coldly. 'Now take the pail off the guy's head and let's see what he's got to say now.'

Hermann nodded to the little interpreter. Carefully, as if he already knew what he was going to find, he lifted off the pail. Porky gave a little grunt of shocked disapproval, as the SS non-com's face was revealed. It looked a mess. Blood was seeping out of both his mouth and his ears. His cheeks were discoloured and were already beginning to swell while his eyes were blackened and were closing rapidly. He looked lost and helpless and Malone knew instinctively he had lost all desire to fight back. He'd talk all right. He turned to Porky and said, 'Let's go and see if we can bum a cup of coffee. I can't stand the smell in this room any longer.'

Porky nodded his agreement.

Hermann took it all in his stride. He gave them his lopsided cunning grin, still chewing the unlit cigar from one side of his fat-lipped mouth to the other. 'I told ya I could make a mummy talk, didn't I, Captain?' He forgot Malone and his look of disapproval. 'All right, ass-hole, let's start talking turkey now . . .'

The Russians were slaughtering the Hitler Youth kids. They couldn't miss, as drunk as they were. The boys in the short pants, band still playing (though now out of tune), flag-bearer still bravely waving his red banner, were walking straight into their ragged fire. Behind them as they advanced on the Russians, they left behind their dead and dying, some of the latter crying for their mothers like the foolish, hurt little boys that they were in reality.

Hummel and his volunteers could hardly bear to look upon the slaughter. It was too horrible. Mere children being sacrificed in this manner for a cause that was already lost. But it made them redouble their efforts as they pushed and shoved the one-ton torpedo on its two-wheel carriage up to the height from which they would launch the strange weapon at the Russians.

So far they had been lucky. The escaped POWs had turned their attention from them to the Hitler Youth, knowing obviously that the stupid kids were an easier target. But Hummel, sweating with the rest as they continued their slow progress between the trees, which gave them some cover for the time being, knew that sooner or later they would be spotted – and then they'd better be in position or their lives wouldn't be worth much out here in the open.

Now they were some fifty metres from the rise's top. Below, the surviving Hitler Youth were unslinging their weapons – they had carried them over their shoulders so far as if they were on parade – and Hummel guessed their commanders were soon going to order to attack – the poor little bastards! He redoubled his efforts behind the weight of the torpedo, urging his volunteers to even greater efforts. For now it was not only a question of saving his Black Devils trapped in the train, but also preventing any of their so-called rescuers from the terrible blood-letting soon to come.

Ping!

A slug howled off the torpedo. Next to Hummel, pushing mightily with the much younger men, the *Obermaat* yelped with pain and clapped his hand momentarily to his shoulder. Bright-red blood seeped through his tightly clenched finger. 'Shit on the shingle!' he cried. 'They've spotted us, sir.'

They had.

A couple of ragged Russians, still wearing the fur hats of the winter campaign in the East in which they had been captured, were dropping to their knees and firing potshots at the four men pushing the torpedo cart.

Hummel swore. 'Hang on to the cart,' he ordered.

Without waiting to see if they were doing so, he darted forward, unslinging his machine pistol as he did so. He knew he had only one magazine left. He couldn't afford to miss.

He ran, crouching, a dozen metres or so, slugs stitching up the earth around his flying feet. He stopped, trying to stop panting, and aimed, firing from left to right like some cowboy gunslinger from the 'Wild West' films he remembered from his youth. The closest Russian clapped his hand to his forehead and screamed with almost unbearable pain then reeled back. The other rose and tried to make a run for it. Hummel didn't give him a chance. He pressed the trigger hard and emptied the rest of the magazine into the running man's back. Great shreds of bloody flesh were ripped away. He staggered, seemed about to fall, managed another few paces and then sighed as if very weary, and sat down like a man does who is about to sleep. Which the Russian did there and then – for ever.

Hummel wasted no more time. He ran back to the others. Up front the Hitler Youth kids were dropping everywhere as the Russians slaughtered them without mercy. Hummel didn't look; he couldn't bear to. All he knew now was he had to bring this unreasoning murder of the innocents to an end. One final push and the torpedo was balancing on the slope with the panting men who had pushed it there, trying to ignore the bullets now coming their way again. Hastily Hummel opened the spigot which gave access to the propellant. Next to him one of his Black Devils splashed the petrol he had brought with him across the torpedo's steel casing. The little *Obermaat* flicked his lighter. The petrol ignited at once. Hastily they let go. The torpedo on its carriage started to roll and bump its way down the slope, gathering speed all the time.

For a few moments the Russians didn't react. They seemed bemused by the spectacle. The Hitler Youth reacted more quickly. The survivors dropped to the ground among their own pathetic dead. Just in time. The blazing torpedo hit a bump and another. The carriage skewed to the left. Another bump. The torpedo slammed to the ground. Now the propellant blazed in a sudden sheet of angry blue flame. '*Duck!*' Hummel cried.

His men needed no urging. They had seen torpedoes explode before.

A screech. A hiss. Like a giant blowtorch, flame seared the steel casing of the torpedo. The paintwork bubbled and erupted like the ugly symptoms of some loathsome skin disease. Next moment the one ton of explosive that the torpedo contained ignited. A huge crash. It was as if the world was disintegrating. The very earth trembled under the lying men's bodies. Next second the Ivans had disappeared in a sea of flame and smoke and the battle was over . . .

One hour later Skorzeny's hastily commandeered fleet of civilian trucks appeared and the battered little group of the Black Devils and their Salamanders were on their way once more. The scene was set; the actors were in position; the final act of the great drama could commence . . .

Book Four:

End at Remagen

'Dust to dust, they say . . . if they had seen this . . . It is not dust . . . it is a disease, the antithesis of dust. Dust is clean. This is foul. These are the glorious dead.'

Lt. Commander Hummel,
March 1945

One

O nce again the engineers ducked. Another great shell was on its way. They could hear the 4,000lb shell fired from the 'Karl's Howitzer' miles away, heading for the bridge at Remagen. All that morning the Ludendorff Bridge had been under attack by the Germans. At dawn twelve V-2 supersonic rockets launched in Holland had peppered the area around the bridge. Now their places had been taken by this monstrous howitzer. So far the only damage they had caused was to a house some 300 yards off where three GIs eating breakfast washed down with looted Rhine wine had been blown to pieces.

Still the watching engineers, heads ducked against the blast of the next shell to land, were worried, very worried. The reverberations were shaking the bridge badly and due to the shellfire their men had been so far unable to weld a huge plate over the severed main arch. Once that was in place, they felt, as they had just told the two 'Eyes and Ears', the Ludendorff Bridge would be secure. Malone had looked at Porky and asked, a little mocking twinkle in his one eye, 'Shall we tell the Master, Porky . . . That news would cheer him up no end.'

Porky had taken it in good part. He'd answered, 'Just let it lie for the time being, old chap. When the thing collapses—'

At that moment another huge shell had plummeted into

the Rhine several hundreds yards away in a gigantic spout
of wild white water, making the bridge shiver and tremble
like a live thing, and he'd completed his sentence with, '. . .
which seems about to happen at any moment. Then we'll
signal Monty the – er – good news.'

Now, however, the two 'Eyes and Ears' were more
worried about the immediate problem. For it was clear to
them that the shelling and V-2 bombardment were merely
a prelude to the major assault on the bridge. As Malone
stated, 'You don't need a crystal ball, Porky, to figure out
how the Krauts are going to do it. They think they can hold
that wood on our side of the Rhine so that the waterborne
attack, in whatever form it'll come, can be launched from
there and have a straight run to the bridge.'

'Yes. General Hodges of the 1st Army thinks that is their
plan, too, when I called him on behalf of the Master in Spa.'
Porky agreed. 'The problem is, as he sees it, when do we
attack the wood and root out the SS Johnnies?'

'Yeah, I've thought about that, too, Porky.' Far away
the huge howitzer thundered again and behind them, appre-
hensive engineer officers, observing the vital bridge's
performance under this horrific barrage, tensed, ducking
their heads deeper into the collars of their greatcoats as if
that might protect them from what was to come.

Malone sniffed contemptuously. 'I guess General Hodges
is inclined to wait and see what happens when these
Skorzeny guys turn up, nipping the whole bunch in the
bud if he can.'

'Yes, that seems to be his plan. Attack the whole bunch
of the Boche together. If it—'

The rest of his words were drowned by another 'Karl's
Howitzer' shell falling out of the sky like a hound of hell.
Again it landed well away from the bridge, though it did
shake the structure violently once more and made Porky

say in his best British stiff-upper-lip manner,' I say, old bean, I think it might be wiser to move away from what I believe the papers back home are now calling "the most famous bridge in the world", what.'

'Too frigging true,' Malone agreed with all the urgency of the New World. 'A guy could get killed here, ya know.'

So they left, leaving behind the engineer officers, white-faced and a little shaky, watching them run to their jeep with undisguised envy. Ten miles away the sweating muscle-bound German gunners began to load yet another 4,000lb shell into the great towering mortar, as if the Führer himself was watching their every movement. Which, in a way, was true. For now Adolf Hitler had taken over personal command of the destruction of the bridge that was named after the general who had once been one of his closest allies in the days when the infant Nazi Party had been struggling for its very existence; and despite the fact that he was virtually senile and a very sick man, he had regained faith in his destiny to stop the rot and still save Germany in what he called now her 'eleventh hour'. He'd surprise General Hodges, commander of the 1st US Army. He'd throw in his '*Kampfschwimmeren*' – 'battle swimmers' – before the main attack went in and then he'd see just how the *Ami* commander would cope with the last of his 'wonder weapons' with which he had promised the German people he could still win the war for the Third Reich . . .

They were all 'old hares', Hummel could see that: tough veterans who had been trained initially by the Italian experts when Italy had still been on the side of the Third Reich. Now they listened attentively as Skorzeny briefed them on the overall plan and the part they'd play

143

in it; while Hummel watched and told himself the Viennese giant was really sending them to their deaths. Not that that worried him.

'The Führer personally has devised this operation,' Skorzeny was saying. 'It is vital to the future of the nation. Each of you will be given an empty petrol can. It will contain nothing but air to give you buoyancy. However, attached to the side of each can there will be four packages of a new Tommy explosive, which we have developed further. It is called "Plastit". It is waterproof, perfectly harmless in its inert phase until you press a pencil charge into it.'

Hummel's eyes narrowed. He had heard of the English-invented explosive, which was totally different from the highly dangerous dynamite and nitroglycerine normally used in these kinds of ops.

'Attach the Plastit to any surface you like – metal, wood, stone – it will stick, set the time pencil and depart, knowing that you won't have been heard. There'll be none of the usual drilling holes to put the charges in. Indeed, I can assure you, comrades, that this will be one of the easiest operations you have ever undertaken.' He beamed at them.

The old hares' tough faces relaxed a little as if they had been convinced by what the commando leader had just said. Hummel didn't. The 'old hares' had been trained in warm seas – the Med, and later the Black Sea when they had carried out missions in Russia. They'd forgotten just how cold northern waters such as the Rhine were. They had the new-fangled websuits, admittedly. But over the hours they might be in the river delivering and attaching their charges to the bridge, the iciness of the water would permeate them and then they'd be fighting not just the enemy but the frightening effect of the cold. He ought to know;

he'd been through similar situations more than once and he hadn't liked them one bit. He waited now to see if Skorzeny would make any reference to the coldness of the water they would soon be facing. He didn't.

Instead he said, 'Comrades, there's rum and hot tea waiting for you outside. There's hot pasta for energy as well if you want it.' Then he surprised Hummel by clicking to attention and raising his hand to the peak of his cap in salute, snapping formally as if one parade, 'Comrades, I salute you. In the name of our Führer, Adolf Hitler, and my Hunting Bands, I thank you. *Hals und Beinbruch.*' And with that, he dismissed them.

Hummel waited till the men he now thought doomed had closed the door of the little riverside cottage behind them before he spoke. He came straight to the point. 'Obersturm,' he snapped harshly, 'why send them on this sortie? They won't make it. It will be a wasted mission and they'll probably be killed.' He added, as if speaking to himself, thinking of the dead kids in the short black pants on that hillside, 'And there have been too many killed *purposelessly* already.'

If Skorzeny noted the criticism in the haggard young naval officer's tone, he didn't comment on it. Instead he said, 'It's all part and parcel of the plan, Kapitänleutnant.' He smiled, as if willing Hummel to agree with him.

The latter wasn't impressed by Skorzeny's attempt to turn on that fake charm that seemed to be part of the make-up of the average Viennese. 'What plan?' he barked.

'To ensure that nothing goes wrong with the main assault,' Skorzeny answered easily. Outside, the front was settling down for the night and the great gun had ceased its thunder so that they could hear the soft chatter of the men as they drank their hot tea-and-rum and ate before the operation commenced. 'They might pull it off, but if they—'

145

'They won't pull it off,' Hummel interrupted him gruffly. 'The Rhine is too cold even for old hares like they are. Even if they aren't forced to give up the mission before they reach the bridge, they won't be of any use when and if they get there. Their limbs will be too numb. They won't be able to attach the plastic explosive. Even setting the time pencil will take major effort.' He shook his head, as if in despair. 'But most probably they won't reach the bridge, as I've said.'

Skorzeny's fake smile had vanished, but still he didn't exhibit any anger. It was as if he were speaking to someone particularly obtuse and it was no use becoming angry with a person of that kind. 'My dear Hummel,' he said slowly, 'don't you see? Those men will prove a diversion if nothing else whatever becomes of them and their mission.'

'*A diversion?*'

'Yes. It will give – your mission – a chance to cross the river this night undetected and link up with my stout fellows of the SS Parachute Regiment. It is unfortunate that they may have to die, but –' again he shrugged in that expressive Viennese manner – 'as they say, you can't make an omelette without breaking eggs.'

Hummel was momentarily so shocked he couldn't respond or react. He gaped at the scarfaced giant as if he couldn't believe the evidence of his own ears. Finally he gasped, 'Surely you can't be serious, *Obersturm*! You can't sacrifice good old hares like that . . . men who have done their utmost for Germany's cause . . . what's the point . . .' The words died on his lips. For he saw that Skorzeny wasn't really listening to his protestations. The decision had already been made and it was final. He was simply wasting his words.

Skorzeny smiled as if he believed by ending his protest so abruptly, the young commander had seen reason and knew that it all had to be done. 'I would guess,' he said, voice all sweet reason and goodness, 'those brave comrades who will soon be swimming down the Rhine will know and approve of the sacrifice that they may well be called upon to make. With the *Amis* preparing to attack into the heart of our beloved Reich, they must realize that no sacrifice is too great.'

Abruptly, Hummel was siezed by a great rage. Perhaps it stemmed from that dawn in a burning Hamburg and the sight of his beautiful dead wife's head in the hatbox; perhaps the rage was occasioned by the terrible slaughter of the Hitler Youth kids the previous day; perhaps it came from a long war with too many dead and too much destruction. For suddenly he found himself intoning in a voice he didn't recognize as his own: 'Dust to dust, they say . . . But if they had seen this, the dead, they wouldn't be able to say those words with such an easy conscience . . . It is not dust . . . war and death in battle . . . *it is a disease*! This is foul . . . these are your glorious dead . . .' Suddenly his voice broke, as if he had just realized what he was saying and he finished with a kind of dry sob, and a question that he knew would never be answered now, 'Oh God, why? . . .'

Skorzeny gave him a hard look. For a moment he hesitated, then on a sudden impulse he pulled out a silver hip flask. 'Best French cognac. The Führer's own private stock. Take a drink. It'll pull you out of your mood.'

Hummel shook his head; he didn't trust himself to speak.

Skorzeny's hard look grew more pronounced. He said, putting away the flask, 'Remember, the Führer ordered and planned this operation personally. I am sure he will resort to most severe measures if anyone fails him in the course of the operation. You'd better be quite clear about that, Hummel.' The threat was all too obvious. Hummel, wasn't impressed. He knew already he was going to die; for at that moment the young officer realized that he had been awaiting death for a long time now. All that mattered now till death occurred was the safety and future of his young men, who, come what may, would be a defeated Germany's future in the hard bitter years to come.

Skorzeny clicked his heels together and came to the position of attention. 'Remember what I have just said to you, Hummel. Now get back to your men and give them their last orders. Your part of the operation commences at zero one hundred hours. Dismiss.' This time Skorzeny didn't give his best wishes as he had done to the 'battle swimmers'.

Nor did Hummel salute, as regulations stipulated he should have done. Indeed anyone watching them at that moment might well have told himself they were the most deadly of enemies. But as the harshly handsome young officer disappeared into the darkness, he had already forgotten Skorzeny and the brutal evil that he represented. His mind was made up. He knew now what he had to do.

Two

One by one the 'battle swimmers' slipped almost noiselessly into the Rhine. On the bank, their helpers handed them the cans to which the plastic explosive was attached. Then they pushed off, following each other in a ragged line, keeping close to the bank for the time being. But Hummel, crouched there, could already hear their muffled gasps of shock as they felt the coldness of the water. He frowned. The trouble was beginning almost immediately and at that moment he wished he could order them back. But he knew he daren't; that would compromise his own plan to save his young volunteers. The 'old hares' would have to fend for themselves the best they could. If they were smart, they'd surrender the first time they were challenged by some *Ami* sentry. But that wasn't to be.

Slowly they allowed themselves to drift to the centre of the river, conserving their strength, knowing that they would need all the energy they could summon up for the final stage of their daring mission – if they ever got that far. Hummel watched them go as long as he could see them. Then they vanished into the chilly March gloom and he rose to his feet to make his own last preparations.

Now all was silent save the soft ripple of the river and solemn hoot of an owl in the tall willows bordering the Rhine. The world had gone to sleep, or so it seemed. But as Hummel walked back slowly over the soggy turf to where his own craft were anchored he knew that wasn't the case. There were men both German and American alert everywhere. Indeed the night was full of impending danger and he knew that he couldn't let his guard down one moment; and it was not only the Americans who might wreck his plan. It could be Skorzeny and his SS fanatics, too. For he guessed that by now the Viennese commando was suspicious of him and would be keeping his eye open for what he would call the first sign of Hummel's treachery. He, Hummel, would have to play the role that Skorzeny expected him to play to the very last moment . . .

Fortunately for the battle swimmers, the half-moon which had now risen was casting its spectral light on the far bank of the Rhine so that they felt they were safe enough in the centre of the river. Here, too, they'd be safe from any sharp-eared enemy soldier who might catch the slight noise they made with their rubber flippers as they propelled themselves along.

But by now they were beginning to feel the effects of the cold water. The warmth created by the hot tea and rum had worn off. A freezing, bone-chilling cold was beginning to penetrate their wetsuits right to the very marrow. How they longed to propel themselves forward vigorously and engender some warmth! But that couldn't be. Hectic swimming caused noise and for the moment noise and the subsequent alarm it might raise among their enemies on both banks were the greatest dangers the battle swimmers faced.

So valiantly they swam on at a measured, slow pace, propelling their charges attached to the cans in front of themselves with hands that were commencing to harden into rigid frozen claws . . .

Hummel rose from the reeds. Carefully he looked to left and right. Nothing. The night was really quiet now.

The battle swimmers had long since vanished and so far they had apparently not hit trouble. At least there had been no firing. He waited, staring now at the opposite bank on the American side of the Rhine where the SS paras were dug in in their hiding places. Two hours before they had sent a coded radio signal to Skorzeny's cottage-based HQ that everything was running smoothly in their forest lair and that apparently the *Amis* had not tumbled to the fact that they had a Trojan Horse in their midst. However, one of their two-man machine-gun teams was missing, but it didn't seem to worry the battalion commander. As he had signalled, 'Patrols often get lost in battle conditions.'

A worried Hummel hoped he was right. He knew that if he and his Black Devils were caught in a river crossing of the kind they were soon going to undertake, it would be total slaughter; they would be sitting ducks.

For they were going to tow the Salamanders across by means of a rope strung over the Rhine. They had worked out that the noise of the Salamanders might well alert the Americans in advance and give the game away before they could start the actual attack. Much now depended upon the SS paras completing that job without too much noise so that the Salamanders could be stowed and armed on the far side of the river, ready for the great assault on the bridge at Remagen.

Suddenly, startlingly, the signal lamp commenced winking on and off on the far bank. Immediately Hummel forgot his fears and foreboding, his own plan pushed to the back of his mind. Next to him, his own signaller started to give the response, while Hummel did his best to note the exact position of the SS's signal. For it would be there where the tow rope would be anchored.

Now time was of the essence. As the signal vanished and the Black Devils, hidden in the reeds with their gear, tensed and waited for their orders, Hummel made one last survey of the immediate area of the Rhine. Everything seemed quiet, almost, as he had thought before, as if the front had gone to sleep. In the distance he could see the occasional signal flare surging into the inky blackness of the night sky, but he told himself they were probably occasioned by nervous sentries, who were seeing intruders everywhere; young sentries, new to the front, were like that.

He was satisfied. He turned to his volunteer. A tough young Black Devil, who was the best young swimmer of his class. 'All right, Fritz,' he whispered, 'off you go. Take care and make a run for it if anything goes wrong – which it won't, of course.'

'Of course, sir,' the boy answered dutifully. Without a second's hesitation, he slipped into the water, bearing the heavy burden of the tow rope over his shoulders. On the German bank, the others under the command of the now patched-up *Obermaat* held on firmly to their end of the heavy tow, digging their feet into the wet mud of the reed beds, and prepared to take the strain. The first stage of the operation was under way . . .

'It's *too* quiet,' the young US artillery officer said softly. 'For days the Krauts have been attempting to knock that damned bridge over there out,' he indicated the Remagen Bridge with the stem of his pipe, 'and now it's as still as the grave. If I were a suspicious man, I'd think the Heinies were up to something.'

Malone, Porky and the artillery captain stood on the height just above the Ludendorff Bridge, where a new battery of artillery, complete with strange-looking search-lights that the two 'Eyes and Ears' couldn't quite make out, were now located.

It was very late, but the two young officers had dozed

all afternoon, after making their morning report to Montgomery's HQ by radio so that they could cover the protection given to the vital bridge during the night hours. The 'Master' had an insatiable desire to know facts so that he could upstage American commanders with details of their dispositions etc. that perhaps even they didn't know.

Thus it was that Porky remarked as they started to stroll reflectively back to the dug-in guns, 'They're funny-looking lights, Captain. Never seen that kind before.'

The young officer chuckled and took his pipe out of his mouth again – like most young pipe-smokers he paid a great deal of attention to his new briar pipe, using it a lot to emphasize his points. Malone guessed he might well have been a college associate prof or something like that before he joined the service. 'I'm not surprised, Captain,' he said. 'Because they're top secret. Haven't been used in Europe till now. We're the first outfit in the E.T.O.* to be equipped with them.'

'Say on, old bean,' Porky encouraged the American, sucking on his pipe like a greedy baby might its mother's breast.

'They're called C.D.L.s,' the young captain continued, 'Canal Defense Lights to you gentlemen. I think they might have been developed for the protection of the Panama Canal against would-be saboteurs – anyway that's my guess.'

'But what's so special about them?' Porky asked.

'This. They throw out a powerful beam of light, but you can't detect its source and attempt to knock out the searchlight with firepower, for example.'

'Sort of like "Monty's Moonlight",' Porky said.

* European Theater of Operations.

153

'Never heard of it,' the American confessed.

'Well,' Porky explained, 'you bounce off the beams of searchlights from clouds somewhere to your front and the light is then directed downwards so that you can give your advancing troops some sort of light at night without revealing its source. Monty's going to use it when we cross the Rhine in a couple of weeks.' He winked at Malone. 'But *we've* already crossed the Rhine, haven't we, Captain—' He stopped short. His bantering tone had changed when he spoke again; it was replaced by one of alarm. 'Christ there's someone down there in the river. I think—'

'Shut up!' Malone interrupted him harshly. He cocked his head to one side and listened. Porky stopped puffing and did the same. For a moment he heard nothing save the soft rustle of the night wind through the girders of the bridge. Then, yes, there it was. A soft movement of water. 'Balls of fire!' he hissed. 'You're right – there is someone down there in the water!' He turned hurriedly. 'Sergeant Petersen,' he ordered swiftly. 'Hit the lights – at the double, man!'

There was a harsh metallic click. A rush of electric power and abruptly, the cold night air was warm. Power increased and the two 'Eyes and Ears' could see the first searchlight crew turning the wheel which swung their top-secret apparatus around. But although the sudden heat indicated electric power and light, the two observers could detect no beam. Yet down below on the Rhine a sudden circle of icy-white light had appeared out of nowhere. A moment later it was joined by another – and then yet another.

Now the strange new lights circled the surface of the Rhine east of the bridge, weaving their intricate patterns until it happened. They coned a solitary figure, pushing something in front of him through the water. '*Got him!*'

the young artillery officer exclaimed in triumph. 'There's the saboteur S.O.B.!' Even before he could shout an order to obtain, his eager young gunners went to work.

Tracer ziz-zagged in a lethal morse across the Rhine. A .50-inch calibre heavy machine gun commenced firing. Its big slugs ripped the water apart. Little angry spurts of white went up in sudden haste. A line of fire headed straight for the first of the 'battle swimmers'. He let go of the can. He tried to dive. But he was too cold and weak to manage it in time. Even at that distance they heard his dying scream of agony as the heavy machine gun ripped his head off and the headless corpse went under, leaving the ghastly rubber-hooded head with its monstrous goggles to bob up and down in a frightening stare of reproach before it drifted away into the outer darkness.

Now the gunners went to work with a will. There were cries of *'There's another of the bastards . . . over there, got him? . . . knock the shit out of the Kraut asshole . . .'* as if this was some back-home country turkey shoot and it was all some great game of fun.

Another battle swimmer was hit. He flung up his arms and went under without a sound. In front of him his Plastit drifted harmlessly underneath the Ludendorff Bridge.

'Kamerad . . . Kamerad!' the plaintive appeal rang up from the water. *'Nicht schiessen . . . oh, bitte nicht schiessen . . . !'* Now encircled in a bright ring of light, Porky and Malone could see the swimmer waving his arms and frantically attempting to surrender before it was too late.

That wasn't to be. Behind them the machine-gunner cried sadistically, 'Let me have him, boys . . . please . . . I ain't killed me a Kraut in this war yet . . .' The others ceased firing and the machine-gunner took careful aim, while down below the unsuspecting German still waved

his arms and hoped that his appeal would work. It didn't.
Next moment the American gunner pressed his firing
button. The heavy machine gun exploded in his grip. The
gleaming belt of ammunition sped through the chamber.
Empty brass cartridge cases tumbled to the ground in
metallic profusion. Below, the trapped battle swimmer
was ripped to pieces. Gory chunks of his torn flesh flew
in all directions. Instantly the water around the man was
transformed a blood red. In a matter of seconds there was
nothing left of him save those pieces of meat looking like
offal left over from the slaughter yard and at the gun the
crazy gunner was crying, 'Christ on the Cross, did you see
that . . . I really ripped that Kraut apart, didn't I, boys.
Wow, wasn't that something!'

As the last battle swimmer slipped noiselessly and unhurt
beneath the surface of the Rhine dead from the cold and
exhaustion, Porky and Malone turned away sickened by
the inhuman slaughter. Beneath his breath, Porky, who
had seen much of war, muttered, 'God in heaven, when
it is all going to end . . . ?' Next to him, Malone, his
normally ruddy face a ghastly pale colour, knew well
what he meant.

Three

Montgomery was feeling quite perky. After the most recent signals from his two 'Eyes and Ears' at the damned Ludendorff Bridge site, he felt his black mood of depression vanishing. Now, although he was indulging in nothing stronger than his nightly glass of warm milk, he felt slightly tipsy, as if he were imbibing the strong waters that his partner on the other end of the line in London was undoubtedly drinking at this particular moment. He said in that squeaky voice of his, pronouncing his Rs like Ws in the upper-class fashion, 'It really looks, Prime Minister, as if the bridge won't last much longer. It's been under German attack all day – the latest is an attempt by Boche frogmen, which unfortunately failed. Now, as I have been informed by some of my young gallopers –' he meant his 'Eyes and Ears' – 'the Boche will launch an all-out assault on the bridge and that, sir, will be that.'

'Careful, Monty,' Churchill in London admonished the Army Group Commander, 'I know this phone is scrambled and secure, but you must remember you are speaking of our allies, the Americans.' Churchill cleared his throat as if in irritation, and Montgomery could visualize the old man taking a swift sip of whatever the strong water was which he was currently drinking this night.

'Of course, sir, I know. But you must remember that the Yanks, especially Eisenhower, are rank amateurs when it

157

comes to strategy. How else could they put all this effort into a blind alley – an attack out of Remagen into bloody nowhere?'

Churchill chuckled softly. He could hear just how rattled Monty was; he rarely cursed.

'Remember, Monty, for every soldier we can field, the Americans field three. In a way they are the bosses now.'

'That may be so, sir,' Monty replied testily, for he had little sense of humour or irony. 'But their numbers don't give them the right to lose the fruits of victory, namely the push into the Ruhr and to the German capital. We must secure Berlin before the Russians. That's what the war is about now. The Germans are defeated already. The Russians are now the potential new enemy.'

'True, true, my dear Field Marshal,' Churchill sighed like a sorely tried man. 'We may think such thoughts, but we must not air them aloud.' He decided he'd humour his army commander a little. 'When this silly little sideshow at Remagen is over, I shall come and visit you in Germany. I want to be in at the kill, if you will permit me. I have, I must confess, a great desire to piss in the German Rhine.'

Monty conceded a point, though he hadn't the slightest intention of letting the Prime Minister – with his childish delight in battle and glory as if he were still a young subaltern of lancers charging at Omdurman – get in the way of his operations. 'Sir, you shall indeed urinate in the Rhine if that is your wish, once we cross. But first we must stop this foolishness at Remagen.'

Churchill gave in. 'I shall use any remaining influence I have with the Supreme Commander to urge him not to reinforce the sideshow, as you call it, Monty, at Remagen. But, I'm afraid, Eisenhower is a tool of his generals and US public opinion. They and it want America to be seen as winning this war, not the British Empire.'

'Damned politics—' Montgomery began, then bit back his words. After all, the man he was speaking to was a politician, too.

'Yes, I know.' For an old man, Churchill's hearing was still very acute; he hadn't missed Montgomery's little outburst. 'But politics are a fact of life.' He yawned. 'Now my dear Monty, I must let you get to bed. I know you retire early. One last thing, however, I beg you.'

'Sir?'

'Whatever happens in the next few days, please do not forget me. Let me have the pleasure of pissing in the Rhine at last . . . Good night, my dear Field Marshal.' The phone went dead.

Montgomery was alone with his glass of milk, already cold, and his thoughts. They weren't pleasant, *now* . . .

Nearly a hundred miles away, Hummel stood on the banks of the Rhine, and waited till the SS Para Battalion Commander had finished urinating into the great river. By now the three Salamanders had been towed across, were anchored and hidden among the reeds till they were needed. The operation had gone off smoothly, but had been broken off temporarily when the wild firing had commenced further up the river close to their objective, the bridge. Automatically the SS troopers and the Black Devils had ceased working. They'd known straight off what had happened: the diversion being used to mask their own crossing to the far bank had ended in disaster. The battle swimmers had gone to their deaths, as Hummel had expected they would.

'Brave fellows,' the hard-faced SS Commander had commented. 'Now then, let's get on with it and ensure that their sacrifice was not in vain.' The youths, both SS and Navy, had redoubled their efforts, while Hummel had told himself that such fine German boys ought – and would – be saved. Even their enthusiasm and effort for a cause that was already lost showed them to be the best types: types that a future Germany couldn't afford to lose in wild adventures such as this hopeless last-minute attack on the Ludendorff Bridge. The shooting of the battle swimmers had strengthened his resolve to do what he'd planned. He had no doubt that it would mean his own death, but that no longer mattered; the fate of the youths did.

The para officer did up his flies. 'Shitting running water,' he growled. 'Always has the same effect on me.' He laughed drily in the fashion of those 'old hares' who were capable of making fun of themselves and everything else for that matter.

For a moment or so, Hummel was tempted to entrust him with his plan. With a bit of luck and skill he might be able to get his paras back across the Rhine before the balloon went up. Then the young naval commander thought again. The paratrooper might agree to make the attempt – he looked like a man who didn't really want to lose his life at this stage of the war – but what about his men? Would they follow suit? Among them there would be the usual blinded fanatics who would feel it an honour to still die for 'Folk, Fatherland and Führer'. No, he dismissed the thought. He would have to do this alone. The paras would have to work out their own solution, if there was one, which Hummel doubted.

'All right, Hauptsturm,' Hummel got on with it. 'This is the drill which I worked out two hours or so ago with Obersturmbannführer Skorzeny.'

'Carry on.'

'As you've already been instructed, you will start a diversion to draw attention away from the river.'

'*Jawohl.* A feint on both the left and right flanks. It

commences at first light when conditions will be in our favour. We try to contain the *Amis* for at least half an hour. Thereafter you're on your own, Kapitänleutnant.'

'Yes, understood,' Hummel lied glibly. 'Then my three Salamanders should be in position and it'll be up to us. However, there has been a slight change in the plan.'

'Change?'

'Nothing of great importance that will affect your op, Hauptsturm,' Hummel responded swiftly. 'It is this. I shall take the first Salamander out personally and alone fifteen minutes before you kick off your feint. That way I'll be in position to guide my youngsters into the attack once they follow'.

It was clear that the SS officer was not convinced by the apparent change in plan. Although Hummel couldn't make out the look on the man's face, he could sense his doubts. Finally he said, 'But won't the noise your – er – Salamander will make give you away? I thought that was the object of the whole exercise – the noise made by my feint would conceal the noise made by your craft?'

'A kind of primitive silencer is to be tried on my Salamander – it's the only one we have been given,' Hummel lied on. 'If we keep the Salamander at – say – two kilometres an hour speed, the noise level is supposed to be very low indeed.' He raised his voice a little. 'If it doesn't work, I've been ordered by Obersturmbannführer Skorzeny to smile gamely and make a pretty corpse.'

The paratrooper chuckled. It was the tough kind of gallows humour that he and his kind of old hare understood. '*He* would say that,' he said and, taking out a crumpled pack of cigarettes, added, 'Go on, have a cancer stick. I think this is no time to be worrying about our health, do you?'

Hummel took one and agreed. Silently he gave a sigh of relief. He'd convinced the paratrooper. Now he was on his own . . .

Crack! The blood-red flare shot out from the trees, arched into the sky and exploded in a burst of colour, flushing the ugly white pre-dawn sky. For a moment the GIs on sentry go in the ruined hamlet some 500 yards away gazed upwards, faces surprised and flushed with the glowing unnatural light. It was as if they couldn't believe the evidence of their own eyes. What in Sam Hill's name was going on?

A moment or two later, they found out. As the dying flare started to descend like a fallen angel, there was the belch and sudden obscene howl of a mortar bomb being fired. A second or so afterwards, the first one came hurtling out of the sky. With elemental fury, it crashed down outside the nearest cottage. The remaining tiles came slithering down in a stone avalanche and the sentry on patrol outside reeled against the wall, hands clasped to a ruined face which looked as if it had had a handful of strawberry jam flung at it.

Suddenly, startlingly, all was chaos and panicked confusion as bomb after bomb came raining down, and close by twin machine guns opened a vicious fire, covering the camouflage-uniformed figures stalking out of the woods, firing from the hip as they did so, crying that frightening battle-cry of the Armed SS – '*ALLES FUR DEUTSCH-LAND!*'

The paras' feint had begun and in the company headquarters near the hamlet's ruined church, the telephones started to jingle and before the lines were cut, a panicked company commander was yelling at the duty clerk in the Ninth's Remagen HQ: 'Krauts . . . hundreds of the

162

S.O.B.s . . . attacking everywhere. We need—' Then the line went dead.

Frantically Porky and Malone slipped into their outer clothing and pulled on their boots.

Outside, the firing was rising to a crescendo and even without being told, the two young officers knew that the SS had attacked out of the wood where they had hidden. That could mean only one thing. As Malone expressed it, checking his .45 Colt now for an extra magazine, 'The Krauts are going for the bridge.'

'Yes,' Porky panted, red-faced with the effort of pulling on his black felt GI overshoes, 'and that's where we're going. The Ninth'll take care of the Jerry paras. We'll get on to the men guarding the bridge.'

Malone had time enough to give him a smile. He said, barely able to conceal his admiration for the fat Englishman, 'Why, you cunning old bird! You want us to keep that bridge after all, don't ya? Monty's gonna have to do his own thing afterwards.'

'Of course,' Porky grunted, getting the left boot on at last, 'we're on the same bloody side, aren't we?'

'You betcha,' Malone yelled, voice full of new hope and enthusiasm. Moments later they were outside in the dawn cold, flinging themselves into the jeep. In the distance, barely noticeable in the hard snap-and-crack of the new fire fight, there was a soft humming noise, getting ever closer . . .

Four

S ince they had captured the SS NCO and convinced him
that he should talk, Malone and Porky had felt they
knew pretty well what the German plan of attack was to
be. Now as Porky braked to a halt on the height where
the artillerymen were dug in, they were caught completely
by surprise. The Germans had done something that they
had not anticipated at all. From somewhere beyond the
hill on the eastern bank of the Rhine, their artillery had
commenced firing smoke shells all around the Ludendorff
Bridge; and it was obvious that one of the SS in the
wood was spotting for them now. For the shells were
straddling both sides of the river approach to the bridge
pretty accurately. Indeed an effective smoke screen was
beginning to form, muting the throbbing slow sound of the
approaching craft.

'Damn and blast,' Porky gasped, reaching for the binoculars dangling from his neck to get a proper view of the
screen, 'the buggers have gone and caught us with our
knickers down!'

'You can say that again, buddy,' Malone said bitterly.
'Right down about out frigging ankles! . . . Come on!' He
grabbed the carbine from the saddle bucket next to the
jeep's driving seat and started for the bridge. 'Let's take
a gander at what's going on down there.'

Porky hesitated a moment. 'That bridge looks none too

164

safe,' he objected. 'The whole structure's shaking again. The shelling's no good for it.'

'Forget it,' his old comrade said. 'If it took your weight, Porky, yesterday, it'll survive a bit longer.' And with that he set off at a smart pace, zig-zagging and occasionally coming to a halt as the smoke shells exploded nearby and sent fresh smoke rising to join the ever-increasing screen.

Hummel kept close to the German side of the Rhine. His brain was racing wildly, as he considered the full implications of his plan. All around him was noise and confusion, yet the lone man in the Salamander did not seem to notice. He was too engrossed in his own thoughts.

He knew, as he had already planned, that once he had been spotted and perhaps dealt with by the enemy gunners, the other members of the Black Devils wouldn't make their own attempts to attack the bridge. After all he was their commander and the one who gave the orders; now there'd be no one to give those orders.

At the same time, although he knew his mission was suicidal, should he simply let himself be killed like some dumb animal without achieving something through his selfless act? Naturally he was saving his young men for Germany's future. But was his life so worthless that he had to throw it away simply for others? Could he – should he – not go out in a blaze of surprise glory? All his young life he had been brought up in the Nazi creed to believe that the ideal end for a young German was the *Heldentod*, the heroic death, for his country. The Führer at those great Party rallies at Nuremberg before the war had always ranted on and on about the willingness to die for a great cause.

Although Hummel knew he had long given up believing in such nonsense, he still had that sneaking feeling of how to go out, blasted into little pieces as was his intention, having done something, perhaps even something spectacular. The damned *Amis* and Tommies had ruined his life that terrible July day in 1943 in Hamburg. Perhaps he ought to take some of them with him, show them that, to the very end, they would have to pay a price for their conquest of his native country.

Suddenly he was seized by a wild unreasoning lust to kill. It was like a raging fire within him; he had never experienced such a feeling before. Hitherto he had always been cool and calculating in his missions. Now he was seized by a kind of euphoria he couldn't explain. Indeed he didn't want to explain it. It would suffice to carry him to his certain death in a mood of joy and exhilaration.

Automatically he adjusted the trim pump. The Salamander raised itself slightly out of the water. He turned up the speed. Beneath him the great two tons of high explosive enclosed in best Krupp steel trembled slightly, as if he had been joined by a live thing. It added to his feeling of crazy joy. He bared his teeth and peered at the yellow smoke of the screen being formed all around him. 'Come on . . . come on,' he urged his steed of steel, 'let's do it . . . *Los, dalli!*'

In front of him another salvo of smoke shells hit the water. Great spouts of water rose high in the air. Next instant yellow smoke streamed upwards as he sailed through the crazy maelstrom, laughing wildly like a madman and urging the Salamander on, as if it could understand his demented commands to it.

For an instant there was a break in the wall of yellow smoke before him. He caught a glimpse of the damned bridge, which had brought him here and caused the death of so many young lives. Abruptly he forgot the enemy, the fact that a few moments before he had intended to destroy it to take his revenge on the *Amis* and the Tommies. Now the bridge itself became the enemy. His lips curled into a sneer of hatred, naked unmitigated hatred. 'Damn you,' he called, 'I'll destroy you yet!' He surged on.

In that same break, Captain Malone caught a brief glimpse of the strange craft hurrying towards the bridge. It looked like an airplane, with its pilot in a cockpit at the rear, being propelled through the water at speed, churning up a white wake behind it. For a moment the American could hardly believe the evidence of his own one eye. Then he realized with the instant recognition of a sudden vision that he had spotted the enemy's secret weapon with which the Krauts hoped to destroy the Ludendorff Bridge.

Hastily, without appearing to take aim, he raised and fired the Springfield carbine. In rapid succession he loosed off a magazine. Beneath his feet the bridge was beginning to sway and tremble alarmingly under the impact of the shells exploding all around it.

Porky, torn between saving the bridge by stopping the attacker in his strange-looking craft below, and getting his friend off the Ludendorff Bridge before it collapsed, yelled frantically, 'Come on, Mike, for God's sake, she's going to go at any moment . . . Leave him you crazy Mick—'

His urgent plea was drowned by the sharp, rifle-like report of a rivet head being sheared off from the girder above his head. He flashed a look upwards. One of the hangers began to groan and break in two. An instant later it tumbled to the wildly swaying bridge, which was now swinging up and down as if the structure was made of pliable rubber cable and not solid steel and concrete.

Porky swallowed hard, the yellow smoke swirling upwards once more and enveloping him and his old friend. He caught one last glimpse of Malone, as he thrust a new magazine of ammunition into his carbine, while from below the roar of the Salamander grew ever louder, indicating that it had almost reached the support pillars of the dying structure now. 'Mike!' he cried again, as the American, carbine raised ready to fire, disappeared into the yellow smoke, 'I'm buggering off – *NOW!*'

He started to run. He did so with difficulty. The entire deck was trembling crazily. Everywhere rivet heads, shorn off, were hissing through the smoke like slugs. As he ran, he felt his feet beginning to go. One moment he was pelting downhill, with the timbers splintering like matchwood and dust rising everywhere; the next he was slogging his way upwards, as if climbing some steep hill. Somehow the fat Guards officer managed to keep his balance and continue running, praying that Malone had heeded his last warning and was following him. If he hadn't – it was a thought that the panting, red-faced officer daren't even think to an end . . .

The bullet hit Hummel on the right temple. For a moment or two he had been knocked out. When he had come to, he had found himself slumped in the shattered cockpit. Hastily and in pain he righted himself the best he could. He shook his head and next moment wished he hadn't. The pain waves shot through his body in electric agony. For a brief second he thought he was going to black out. Weakly he wiped the blood from his face and tried to keep control of the Salamander. For the shock waves coming from the bridge were turning the Rhine into a choppy maelstrom, rocking the craft as if it were one of those lightweight sailing boats he had sailed on Hamburg's Outer Alster as an enthusiastic kid.

For a moment he forgot his mission. He was transported back to those sunlit summer days, which seemed to go on for ever: the girls in their yachting caps and tight white trousers; the sparkling water; the sheer pleasure of sailing, cutting and turning, chasing the wind, feeling vainly proud when you outdid some fellow blond enthusiast and the nights in the long grass afterwards. For some reason tears welled into his glazed eyes. Was it pity? Nostalgia? The longing for a lost youth?

'*Stupid piss pansy!*' he growled at himself abruptly, ashamed of this moment of succumbing to weakness. 'Get on with it, you silly piece of dog shit . . . *MARCH OR CROAK!*'

Malone was bleeding badly from the wound on the top of his head. His helmet liner had fallen in the same instant that the girder had sheared off with the grind of tearing metal and hit him on the head. He had reeled and nearly fallen through the gaping hole that had appeared suddenly at his feet down to the Rhine far below. In the very last minute he had steadied himself, teetering as he was on the edge of the hole. Carefully, feeling his body shaking all over, as if he had been seized by a sudden tropical fever, he had stepped back and grabbed hold of the nearest stanchion for support. For what seemed a long time he stood there trembling, trying to calm himself.

All around him there were strange whispering noises, sharp cracks, vibrating metal, dust devils dancing in the cracks of the splintering wooden planking. It felt as if the bridge had a life of its own and was protesting against the unbearable strain being placed upon it.

He knew he was alone. By now it had to be every man for himself. The engineers, the POWs working as labourers, the light anti-aircraft gunners would be all running for their lives. For even the most stupid of those on the bridge knew by now that it was only a matter of minutes before it broke up and sent those still on it plunging to their deaths in the Rhine. Still that knowledge didn't seem to worry him unduly. He knew he had a job to do. What it was, in his dazed condition, he didn't exactly know at that particular moment. But there was something he had to do before he could make a run for it with the rest.

Again there was a wave of new vibrations. The bridge buckled and twisted and heaved like he remembered a road doing in the Mid-West when he had watched a twister cross the flat Kansas plain as a kid. The sight woke him up to his position. He remembered now what he was supposed to do. He was to kill the man in the strange craft down below in the Rhine. But where was his carbine? . . . Christ on a Crutch, where was his goddam Springfield?

A hundred or so yards away, Lt. Commander Hummel was equally confused. He was losing blood rapidly. He felt himself weakening all the time. All the same he knew he must hold on, not let go of the primitive steering apparatus. Through the clouds of rolling yellow smoke, he kept catching glimpses of the bridge – it seemed to be wavering all the time like a mirage seen in a desert – but he knew it was close. If he could only keep going a little longer . . . five minutes . . . perhaps even only a couple . . . 'Please God,' he croaked, 'just one more minute . . .'

Even as he prayed to God, his face was growing ever bigger in the ring sight of Malone's carbine. He too was wavering, rocked back and forth by the swaying of the dying bridge. 'Keep damned still!' he snapped, thrusting the carbine's butt ever tighter into his shoulder, curling his finger around the trigger and taking that first pressure before he pulled it all the way back and blasted that damned Kraut below to all eternity. Then it would be over and he would be able to sit down and rest. For he felt a great, almost overwhelming desire to rest. What he wouldn't give to lie down on the bridge and sleep!'

Sleep, or was it death, was overcoming Hummel too. He was fading fast, though he felt it was just exhaustion. Time and time again his weakened hands slipped and lost control of the Salamander momentarily. Just before it crashed into the bank, he'd grab the wheel again and hold on to it again, as if it were the most important thing in the world to do so.

In a way it was. The two of them, the unknown enemies, Hummel and Malone, were like two heavyweight boxers at the end of some great contest, groggy, bog-eyed, swaying badly and bleeding, staying on their feet by sheer naked willpower – and hate.

But not for much longer.

As Hummel suddenly lost control of the Salamander altogether, the last German shell of the smoke barrage struck it. Violent flame seared the length of the ugly craft. It heaved madly. Great chunks of metal debris flew through the air. Hummel screamed. The sound was almost inhuman, a cry of absolutely unbearable agony. He gasped for air. He fought the darkness which threatened to blind him. He couldn't. A great flash of high explosive. Hummel was thrown up and outwards. He slammed against the pillar of the bridge, it shattered his bleeding stumps of arms outstretched like those of some latterday Christ, his eyes suppurating empty pits oozing purple matter. Slowly, very slowly, his corpse started to slide down into the Rhine, leaving a bloody slime behind it. Then he was gone beneath the surface . . .

Exactly one minute later the Ludendorff Bridge collapsed at last. With frightening suddenness for such a great powerful structure, it slid downwards to vanish too beneath the surface of the water, carrying its dead and dying with it. Malone went too.

Abruptly there was a loud echoing silence, broken only by the obscene belches of the huge air bubbles bursting on the debris-littered water, which was rapidly settling down

Duncan Harding

once more, the only movement now that of the dead bodies floating face down till they vanished finally in the morning gloom. The most famous bridge in the world had gone at last . . .

Harding:

'If God is with us, who can be against us?'

W ell, gentle reader, as you have read, the story of the 'most famous bridge in the world – for a week' was no saga of sweetness and light. Despite the 'all expenses paid' bit, the research for the story at Remagen brought me little personal pleasure. The buxom blonde Gretchens eager to give a middle-aged '*Englander*' a whirl under the '*Federdecke*' seemed to have vanished. But I must confess my first encounter in that dreamy sleepy Rhenish township seemed to herald some kind of a fun time.

I'd gone to view the ruins of that famous bridge. They are still there nearly sixty years on – mainly the couple of red-brick towers from whence Captain Friesenheim, the German engineer officer, had first attempted to blow up the Ludendorff Brucke: I was poking around a bit when I heard the sound of a hammer tapping away behind one of the bridge's remaining supports.

Curious as old hacks are, I went to investigate and found an old guy sitting cross-legged, with several cans of the local *Romerpils* next to him, busily engaged in breaking up new bricks with his hammer. Next to the water's edge he had already placed a neat stack of the newly broken bricks. The sight intrigued me. What purpose was he serving, breaking up the new bricks and stacking the remnants so neatly, as if they were of some value?

Fortunately the old boy knew some English and when

I asked him what he was doing, he grinned, showing a mouthful of gold teeth, and said, '*Andenken* . . . You know – *souvenirs*.' He pointed to the twin towers and I realized the new bricks he was breaking up were of the same dull-red colour and size as the original ones of the vanished bridge.

I got it immediately. I'd seen a little shop near the burgomaster's office where they were selling little books on the famous bridge and bits of brick, enclosed in a frame, bearing the legend 'Original Remagen Bridge Stonework' at twenty euros a piece.

'No more bricks from bridge,' the old boy said and chuckled, probably at the stupid look on yours truly's mug. 'Now we make old new bricks, *Verstehen?*'

'*Verstehen.*' I did. The cunning old bugger had gotten himself a nice little earner. Then with supposedly German industry, he got back to the business of breaking up his bricks to be sold to probably gullible *Ami* tourists. I walked away, telling myself that I had always regarded myself as something of a dyed-in-the-wool cynic. But the old man with his 'new-old bricks' certainly took the biscuit.

After that it all went pretty much downhill. The burgomaster, a nice young chap, received me and told me what he knew of the 'Remagen business' (as he called it in his excellent English), which had 'happened long before I am being born'. He was glad I had come to see him and hoped I would 'tell a nice story'. 'We need the tourists,' he explained. He indicated the line of 'olde worlde' hotels lining the Rhine embankment. 'Business is bad. Germans, they know nothing of the bridge. We need the *Amis* – er Americans. They know the bridge story. It is a famous part of their history.' He sighed and gave an expressive shrug of his shoulders. 'But these days, they are very afraid of bombs, terrorists, aeroplanes.' He shrugged again. I told him they were not the only ones who didn't take kindly to travelling in aeroplanes, especially when they were run by Mick ex-farmers. Again, just before I left, he repeated his request to 'tell a nice story'. I said I'd try.

Well, as you know now, dear reader, it didn't turn out to be a 'nice story' in any shape or form. So many young lives lost that March so long ago so that their sacrifice could become part of the tourist trade and fill those hotels along the waterfront with their menu boards and windows full of bright spring flowers!

As I walked back to the little railway station at Remagen to take the train back to Cologne Airport and the Mick airline, I passed one of the place's turn-of-the-century houses, which still bore the ugly pockmarks of shellfire on its frontage. But it was the framed inscription in Gothic lettering above the house's door which caught my attention. In fact, I even stopped and took a note of the wording so that I could check later that I had translated the inscription correctly. It read: 'If God is with us, then who can be against us?'

Well, I thought, as I trundled myself into the station and headed for its café and a good stiff drink (the 'all expenses' hadn't quite run out yet), in those days so long ago when the ruined bridge down below on the Rhine had occupied the attention of the 'great' from Hitler downwards, God had apparently smiled on no one. Perhaps that March, he had given up on the human race and simply looked the other way?

'Porky', or as he is known now, Sir John Posslethwaite, owner of half of East Yorkshire (or so it seemed to me when I trekked into that savage wild region to interview him on his country estate), appeared to think the same, too. As the taxi dropped me off in front of his eighteenth-century Palladian manor, he was trying to mount a very skittish

177

thoroughbred. The beast wasn't having it, it appeared. It was rearing and bucking, while 'Porky' had just managed to get one foot in the stirrup and I could hear him cursing and snorting, 'If you're bloody well trying to get up here, I'm getting off!' I could tell even then that, although he was very old (well over eighty I would have guessed), he still possessed the same sense of humour that had kept him sane as the fat young Guards officer who had seen his best friend, 'Mike' Malone, perish on the bridge at Remagen.

'We never found him,' he said, toying with his whisky glass in the library of the big house, a splendid wood fire crackling in the big grate and casting wild flickering shadows on the walls. 'We searched for days. But in the end, I had to get back to the Master and carry on with the war.' He sighed softly and I could see the sudden wet sheen in his faded eyes as he remembered those terrible days. 'It was like that then. One didn't have the time to think . . . sorrow for the dead. Perhaps it's better that way.' He rubbed his gnarled knuckles across his eyes for a moment.

There was a long silence then. Somewhere an ancient grandfather clock ticked away the minutes of our life with grave metallic inexorability. The logs crackled. Looking at the old man, who had long given up his chocolate bars and sweets so that he was very frail and thin now, one might have thought he was dead already. But he wasn't.

Suddenly out of the blue, he said in a voice that was now definitely old and reedy, 'You saw the portraits of my ancestors in the Long Gallery as you came through, Harding. Most of them, as you could see, were military men. Coldstreamers for the most part. The Posslethwaites always join the Coldstream. Did well for the most part. One of them even won the Victoria Cross in the Boer War. Posthumously, of course. Like so many of my ancestors . . .

killed leading their company in action . . . rallying a regiment . . . holding the line against overwhelming odds. The citations always read something like that. But always dead.' He frowned, as if his Scotch had suddenly turned very bitter.

'And you think it wasn't worth it?' I jumped in, not really knowing why I asked the question.

He wasn't offended as some of these old toff farts might have been. Indeed he appeared to give the question serious thought. Finally he said slowly, 'Of course I'm proud of them, very proud . . . just as I was of Mike Malone at that bloody bridge. He didn't run away like I did. He stuck it out, although he must have known, the poor bugger, that he was for the chop by doing so. But what was the purpose of it all? What did my ancestors achieve of lasting importance? What did we achieve in that March all those years ago?' Suddenly he sat up, abruptly very alert for such an old man. 'Let me tell you something, Harding, before you go. On that March 7th, 1945, when the Yanks captured the Ludendorff Bridge, Stalin, the Russki dictator, summoned Marshal Zhukov, his senior commander from the front in Germany to Moscow.

'You see Stalin had just heard the Remagen news too. Anyway he told the Russian commander to go hell-for-leather for Berlin before the Yanks broke out of their bridgehead at Remagen and headed for Berlin as well. Well, as you perhaps know, Harding, the Russkis reached Berlin first and out of that supposed Yankee victory there came a very grave defeat for the West. The result was that the Russkis would control Central Europe for the best part of the next forty years. You know, the Cold War and all that.'

His voice grew weak again. He slumped back in his chair, as if he were tired, very tired. 'So what did we

179

achieve at Remagen?' he asked, talking to the dying
flames of the log fire, as if I were no longer present.
He answered his own question, the words hardly audible
now. 'Nothing . . . absolutely nothing really . . .'

I left him sitting there, staring at the fire. I had guessed
he was a courteous man. But he didn't look up when I left
the library or say goodbye. Instead he just slumped there
and I had to look hard a couple of times to check if he
was still breathing. He was, but at that moment he looked
already dead.

It was snowing hard when the servant whistled up the
taxi to take me to Driffield and from there by train to
York, where it looked as if civilization finally had reached
the borders of this remote northern county. 'Expenses'
had run out and I had to travel 'standard'. But I didn't
mind. The train was warm and I had calculated that if I
dispensed with one of GNER's sandwiches, pitched at the
multi-millionaire level, I might be able to afford a double
Scotch. By Bedford, with the snow vanished and still warm
from the double, I was feeling quite optimistic again. I'd
forgotten the 'most famous bridge' and was wondering how
I might sell another one of my 'celebrated novels' to my
publisher. If I could con him with that idea I had for a
story set in the United States, there might be expenses in
it once more. Yes, I told myself, things were looking up
again . . .